Tove Jansson
Moominvalley in November

Translated by Kingsley Hart

PUFFIN

PUFFIN BOOKS

Published by the Penguin Group
Penguin Books Ltd, 80 Strand, London WC2R ORL, England
Penguin Group (USA) Inc., 375 Hudson Street, New York, New York 10014, USA
Penguin Group (Canada), 90 Eglinton Avenue East, Suite 700, Toronto, Ontario, Canada M4P 2Y3
(a division of Pearson Penguin Canada Inc.)
Penguin Ireland, 25 St Stephen's Green, Dublin 2, Ireland (a division of Penguin Books Ltd)
Penguin Group (Australia), 250 Camberwell Road, Camberwell, Victoria 3124, Australia
(a division of Pearson Australia Group Pty Ltd)
Penguin Books India Pvt Ltd, 11 Community Centre, Panchsheel Park, New Delhi – 110 017, India
Penguin Group (NZ), 67 Apollo Drive, Rosedale, North Shore 0632, New Zealand
(a division of Pearson New Zealand Ltd)
Penguin Books (South Africa) (Pty) Ltd, 24 Sturdee Avenue, Rosebank, Johannesburg 2196, South Africa

Penguin Books Ltd, Registered Offices: 80 Strand, London WC2R ORL, England

puffinbooks.com

First published in Finland as *Sent i November* 1971
This translation first published in England by Ernest Benn Ltd 1971
Published in Puffin Books 1974
024

Copyright © Tove Jansson, 1971
English translation copyright © Ernest Benn Ltd, 1971
All rights reserved

Set in Intertype Plantin

Printed in England by Clays Ltd, St Ives plc

British Library Cataloguing in Publication Data
A CIP catalogue record for this book is available from the British Library

ISBN: 978-0-140-30715-3

www.greenpenguin.co.uk

MIX
Paper from
responsible sources
FSC
www.fsc.org   FSC® C018179

Penguin Books is committed to a sustainable
future for our business, our readers and our planet.
This book is made from Forest Stewardship
Council™ certified paper.

PUFFIN BOOKS

Moominvalley in November

Tove Jansson was born in Helsingfors, Finland, in 1914. Her mother was a caricaturist (and designed 165 of Finland's stamps) and her father was a sculptor. Tove Jansson studied painting in Finland, Sweden and France. She lived alone on a small island in the gulf of Finland, where most of her books were written.

Tove Jansson died in June 2001.

Books by Tove Jansson

COMET IN MOOMINLAND

FINN FAMILY MOOMINTROLL

THE EXPLOITS OF MOOMINPAPPA

MOOMINSUMMER MADNESS

MOOMINLAND MIDWINTER

TALES FROM MOOMINVALLEY

MOOMINPAPPA AT SEA

MOOMINVALLEY IN NOVEMBER

TO
MY BROTHER
LASSE

NARRATIVE

CHAPTER I

Snufkin

EARLY one morning in Moominvalley Snufkin woke up in his tent with the feeling that autumn had come and that it was time to break camp.

Breaking camp in this way comes with a hop, skip and a jump! All of a sudden everything is different, and if you're going to move on you're careful to make use of every single minute, you pull up your tent pegs and douse the fire quickly before anyone can stop you or start asking questions, you start running, pulling on your rucksack as you go, and finally you're on your way and suddenly quite calm, like a solitary tree with every single leaf completely still. Your camping-site is an empty rectangle of bleached grass. Later in the morning your friends wake up and say: he's gone away, autumn's coming.

Snufkin padded along calmly, the forest closed round him and it began to rain. The rain fell on his green hat and on his raincoat, which was also green, it pittered and pattered everywhere and the forest wrapped him in a gentle and exquisite loneliness.

There were many valleys along the coast. The mountains rolled down to the sea in long stately curves to promontories and bays which cut deep into the wild country. In one of these valleys a fillyjonk lived all by herself. Snufkin had met many fillyjonks in his time and knew that they had to do things in their own way and according to their own silly rules. But he was never so quiet as when he went past the house of a fillyjonk.

The fence had straight and pointed posts and the gate was locked. The garden was quite empty. The clothes-line had been taken in and the woodpile had gone. There was no hammock and no garden furniture. There was none of the charming disorder that generally surrounds a house in summer, no rake, no bucket, no left-behind hat, no saucer for the cat's milk, none of the other homely things that lie around waiting for the next day and make the house look welcoming and lived in.

Fillyjonk knew that autumn had arrived, and she shut herself up inside. Her house looked completely closed and deserted. But she was there, deep deep inside behind the high impenetrable walls and the dense fir-trees that hid her windows.

The quiet transition from autumn to winter is not a bad time at all. It's a time for protecting and securing things and for making sure you've got in as many supplies as you can. It's nice to gather together everything you possess as close to you as possible, to store up your warmth and your thoughts and burrow yourself into a deep hole inside, a core of safety where you can defend what is important and precious and your very own. Then the cold and the storms and the darkness can do their worst. They can grope their

way up the walls looking for a way in, but they won't find one, everything is shut, and you sit inside, laughing in your warmth and your solitude, for you have had foresight.

There are those who stay at home and those who go away, and it has always been so. Everyone can choose for himself, but he must choose while there is still time and never change his mind.

Fillyjonk started to beat carpets at the back of her house. She put all she'd got into it with a measured frenzy and

everybody could hear that she loved beating carpets. Snufkin walked on, lit his pipe and thought: they're waking up in Moominvalley. Moominpappa is winding up the clock and tapping the barometer. Moominmamma is lighting the stove. Moomintroll goes out on to the veranda and sees that my camping-site is deserted. He looks in the letter-box down at the bridge and it's empty, too. I forgot my goodbye letter, I didn't have time. But all the letters I write are the same: I'll be back in April, keep well. I'm going away but I'll be back in the spring, look after yourself. He knows anyway.

And Snufkin forgot all about Moomintroll as easily as that.

At dusk he came to the long bay that lies in perpetual shadow between the mountains. Deep in the bay some early lights were shining where a group of houses huddled together.

No one was out in the rain.

It was here that the Hemulen, Mymble and Gaffsie lived, and under every roof lived someone who had decided to stay put, people who wanted to stay indoors. Snufkin crept past their backyards, keeping in the shadows, and he was as quiet as he could be because he didn't want to talk to a soul. Big houses and little houses all very close to each other, some were joined together and shared the same gutters and the same dustbins, looked in at each other's windows, and smelt their food. The chimneys and high tables and the drain-pipes, and below the well-worn paths

leading from door to door. Snufkin walked quickly and silently and thought: oh all you houses, how I hate you!

It was almost dark now. The Hemulen's boat lay pulled up under the alders, and there was a grey tarpaulin covering it. A little higher up lay the mast, the oars and the rudder. They were blackened and cracked by the passing of many a summer, they had never been used. Snufkin shook himself and walked on.

But Toft curled up inside the Hemulen's boat heard his steps and held his breath. The sound of Snufkin's footsteps got farther and farther away, and all was quiet again, and only the rain fell on the tarpaulin.

The very last house stood all by itself under a dark green wall of fir-trees, and here the wild country really began. Snufkin walked faster and faster straight into the forest. Then the door of the last house opened a chink and a very old voice cried: 'Where are you off to?'

'I don't know,' Snufkin replied.

The door shut again and Snufkin entered his forest, with a hundred miles of silence ahead of him.

CHAPTER 2

Toft

TIME passed and the rain went on falling. There had never been an autumn when it had rained so much. The valleys along the coast sank under the weight of all this water that was streaming down the hillsides and the ground rotted away instead of just withering. Suddenly summer seemed so far away that it might just as well have never been and the distances between the houses seemed greater and everyone crept inside.

Deep in the prow of the Hemulen's boat lived Toft. No one knew that he lived there. Only once a year in spring was the tarpaulin lifted off and someone gave the boat a coating of tar and tightened the worst cracks. Then the tarpaulin was pulled over again and under it the boat just went on waiting. The Hemulen never had time to take it out to sea and anyway he didn't know how to sail.

Toft liked the smell of tar and he was very particular about living in a place which had a nice smell. He liked the coil of rope that held him in its firm grasp and the unceasing sound of the rain. His big overcoat was warm and a very good thing to have on during the long autumn nights.

In the evening, when everyone had gone home and the

bay was silent, Toft would tell himself a story of his own. It was all about the Happy Family. He told it until he went to sleep, and the following evening he would go on from where he had left off, or start it all over again from the beginning.

Toft generally began by describing the happy Moomin-valley. He went slowly down the slopes where the dark pines and the pale birch-trees grew. It became warmer. He tried to describe to himself what it felt like when the valley opened out into a wild green garden lit by sunshine, with green leaves waving in the summer breeze, the green grass all round him with patches of sunlight in it, and the sound of bees, and everything smelling so nice, and he walked on slowly until he heard the sound of the river. It was important not to change a single detail: once he had placed a summer-house by the river, but it had been a mistake. All that had to be there was the bridge and the letter-box. Then came the lilac-bushes and Moomin-pappa's woodshed, both with their own smells of summer and safety.

It was very quiet and rather early in the morning. Now Toft could see the ornamental ball of blue glass which stood on a pillar at the bottom of the garden. It was Moominpappa's crystal ball and it was the finest in the whole valley. It was a magic ball.

The grass grew tall and was full of flowers, and Toft described them to himself. He told himself about the raked paths neatly bordered with shells and nuggets in gold, and dallied when he came to the little spots of sunlight that he was particularly fond of. He let the wind sigh high above the valley and through the forest on the hillside and then die down again so that the stillness was perfect again. The apple-trees were in bloom. He put apples on some of the

trees, but then took them away again, he put up a hammock and scattered yellow sawdust in front of the woodshed, and now he was quite near the house. There was the peony bed and now came the veranda . . . The veranda lay basking in the morning sun, and it was exactly as Toft had made it, the rail in fretsaw work, the honeysuckle, the rocking-chair, everything.

Toft never went into the house, he waited outside. He waited for Moominmamma to come out on the steps.

Unfortunately, at that point he usually went to sleep. Only once had he caught a glimpse of her nose in the doorway, a round friendly nose, all of Moominmamma was round in the way that mamas should be round.

Now Toft wandered through the valley again. He had done this hundreds of times before and each time the excitement of going over it again became more and more intense. Suddenly a grey mist descended over the landscape, it was blotted out, and he could see only the darkness inside his closed eyes and hear the endless autumn rain falling on the tarpaulin. Toft tried to get back to the valley, but he couldn't.

This had happened quite a few times during the past week and every time the mist descended earlier. The day before it had come down at the woodshed, and now it was already dark by the lilac-bushes. Toft huddled up inside his coat and thought tomorrow perhaps I shan't even get as far as the river. I don't seem to be able to describe things so that I can see them any longer, everything's going backwards.

Toft slept for a while. When he woke up in the dark he knew what he would do. He would leave the Hemulen's boat and make his way to Moominvalley and walk on to the veranda, open the door and tell them who he was.

When Toft had made up his mind, he went to sleep again and slept all night without dreaming.

CHAPTER 3

Fillyjonk

ON Thursday in November it stopped raining and Fillyjonk decided to wash the windows in the attic. She heated
some water in the kitchen and sprinkled a little soap into it,
but only a little, then she carried the bowl upstairs, put it
on a chair and opened the window. Then something came
loose from the window-frame and fell close to her paw. It
looked like a little bit of cotton fluff but Fillyjonk knew
immediately what it was; it was a horrid chrysalis and
inside it was a pale white caterpillar. She shivered and drew
in her paws. Wherever she went, whatever she did, she
always came across creepy-crawly things, they were everywhere! She took her duster and with a quick movement she
swept the chrysalis out watching it roll down the roof,
jump over the edge and disappear.

Horrid, whispered Fillyjonk, and shook out her duster.
She lifted up the bowl and climbed through the window to
wash it from the outside.

Fillyjonk was wearing her carpet slippers and as soon as
she was on the steep wet roof she started to slide

19

backwards. She didn't have time to feel afraid. She flung
her skinny body forwards as quick as lightning, and in a
giddy-making flash slid down the roof on her stomach, her
slippers met the edge of the roof, and there she lay. Now she
was scared. Fear crept through her and stuck like an inky
taste in the throat. She blinked, but her eyes saw the
ground far below, her jaws were locked tight with horror
and astonishment and she couldn't scream.

Anyway, there was no one there to hear her. Fillyjonk
had at last got rid of all her relatives and tiresome acquaintances. She had as much time as she wanted to look

after her house and her solitude and fall off her own roof all by herself among the beetles and indescribable maggots in the garden.

Fillyjonk made an agonized creeping movement upwards, her paws groped over the slippery metal roof but she slid back again and ended up where she had started from. The open window was banging in the wind, the wind sighed below in the garden, and time passed. A few drops of rain splashed on the roof.

Then Fillyjonk remembered the lightning-conductor which went up to the attic on the other side of the house. Very, very slowly, she began to drag herself along the edge of the roof, first a little bit with one foot and then a little bit with the other. With her eyes tight shut and her stomach pressing against the roof, Fillyjonk crawled round her big house and all the time she kept remembering that she suffered from dizziness and what it was like when it came over her. Then she felt the lightning-conductor under her paw, grabbed it for dear life, and with her eyes tight shut, carefully pulled herself up to the floor above; there was nothing else in the whole world now except a thin wire with a fillyjonk suspended from it.

She caught hold of the narrow wooden edging which went round the attic, pulled herself up and lay quite still. Gradually she got up on all fours and waited until her legs stopped shaking, and didn't feel the slightest bit ridiculous. Step by step she began to go a little farther, her face against the wall. She came to window after window, but they were all closed. Her nose was too long and got in the way, her hair fell over her eyes and tickled her nose: I mustn't sneeze, if I do I shall lose my balance ... I mustn't look and I mustn't even think. The heel of one of my slippers is all twisted, nobody cares what happens to me, my corset is all wrinkled up somewhere and any second now of all these awful seconds . . .

It started to rain again. Fillyjonk opened her eyes and saw the steep roof over her shoulder and the edge of the roof and the fall below it through nothing and her legs started to shake again and everything began to go round and round – the dizziness had come. It pulled her away from the wall, the edge she was standing on became as thin and narrow as a razor, and in one interminable second she tumbled all the way back through the whole of her filly-jonkish life. Very slowly she leant backwards, away from safety and towards the inexorable angle at which she would fall, was suspended there for what seemed like another eternity, and then sank forwards again.

Now she was nothing at all, just something that was trying to make itself as flat as possible and move on. There was the window. The wind had slammed it tight shut. The window-frame was smooth and bare and there was nothing there to catch hold of and pull on, not even the smallest little nail. Fillyjonk tried with a hairpin, but it just bent. There inside she could see the bowl with the soapy water and the duster, an impassive picture of a commonplace, an unattainable world.

The duster! It had got caught in the window-frame . . . Fillyjonk's heart began to pound – she could see a little bit of the corner of the duster sticking out, she took hold of it, oh so carefully, and pulled it gently . . . Oh, please don't let it break, let it be my lovely new duster and not the old one . . . I shall never save old dusters again, I shall never save anything again, I shall be extravagant, I shall stop cleaning up, I do too much of it anyway, I'm pernickety . . . I shall be something quite different but not a fillyjonk . . . This is what Fillyjonk thought, imploringly, but hopelessly, be-

22

cause a fillyjonk can never, of course, be anything but a fillyjonk.

The duster held. Slowly the window opened again and the wind banged it against the wall and Fillyjonk flung herself headlong into the safety of the room and lay on the floor and her stomach started going round and round and she felt terribly sick.

Above her head the lamp in the ceiling swayed to and fro in the wind, all its tassels swinging at a uniform distance from one another, each with a little bead on the end. She

looked at them attentively, quite taken by surprise by the little tassels which she didn't remember ever having seen before. And never before had she noticed that the lampshade was red, a very beautiful red reminding her of the sunset. Even the hook in the ceiling had a new and unusual shape.

She began to feel a little better. She began to think how strange it was that everything that hangs from a hook really goes on hanging downwards and not in any other direction, and wondered what it depended on. The whole room had changed, everything looked new. Fillyjonk went up to the mirror and looked at herself. Her nose was covered in

23

scratches on one side and her hair was dead straight and wet through. Her eyes looked different: fancy having eyes to see with, she thought, and how *does* one see . . .?

She began to feel cold because of the rain, and because she had tumbled all the way through her life in a single second, and she decided to make herself a cup of coffee. But when she opened the cupboard in the kitchen, she saw for the first time that she had far too much china. Such an awful lot of coffee cups. Far too many serving dishes and roasting dishes, and stacks of plates, hundreds of things to eat from and eat on, and only one fillyjonk. And who would have them all when she died?

— I'm not going to die at all, whispered Fillyjonk, and shut the cupboard door with a bang. She ran into the living-room, she staggered round among the furniture in her bed-room and out again, she dashed into the drawing-room and drew back the curtains and then went up to the attic, and it was just as quiet everywhere. She left all the doors open, she opened the wardrobe where her suitcase lay, and at last she knew what she was going to do. She would go and stay with someone. She wanted to see people. People who talked and were pleasant and went in and out and filled the whole day so that there was no time for terrible thoughts. Not the Hemulen, not Mymble, certainly not Mymble! But the Moomin family. It was about time that she went to see Moominmamma. You have to decide these things when you're in a certain mood, and quickly, too, before the mood vanishes.

Fillyjonk took out her suitcase and put her silver vase in it, Moominmamma must have that. She threw the water out on to the roof and closed the window. She dried her hair and put it in curlers, and then she drank her afternoon tea. The house had calmed down and was quite itself again.

When Fillyjonk had washed up her tea cup she took the silver vase out of the suitcase and put a china one in instead. She lit the lamp in the ceiling because the rain had made it get dark early.

What on earth came over me, Fillyjonk thought. That lamp-shade isn't red at all. It's a little brownish. But in any case, I'm going away.

CHAPTER 4

Rain

IT was late in the autumn. Snufkin continued towards the
south, sometimes he pitched his tent and let the time pass
as best it might, he walked around and contemplated things
without actually thinking or remembering anything, and he
slept quite a lot. He was attentive but not in the least
curious, and didn't worry much about where he was going
– he just wanted to keep moving.

The forest was heavy with rain and the trees were absolutely motionless. Everything had withered and died, but
right down on the ground the late autumn's secret garden
was growing with great vigour straight out of the mould-
ering earth, a strange vegetation of shiny puffed-up plants
that had nothing at all to do with summer. The late blue-
berry sprigs were yellowish-green and the cranberries as
dark as blood. Hidden lichens and mosses began to grow,
and they grew like a big soft carpet until they took over the
whole forest. There were strong new colours everywhere,

and red rowan berries were shining all over the place. But the bracken had turned black.

Snufkin got a feeling that he wanted to write songs. He waited until he was quite sure of the feeling and one evening he got out his mouth-organ from the bottom of his rucksack. In August, somewhere in Moominvalley, he had hit upon five bars which would undoubtedly provide a marvellous beginning for a tune. They had come completely naturally as notes do when they have been left in peace. Now the time had come to take them out again and let them become a song about rain.

Snufkin listened and waited. The five bars didn't come. He went on waiting without getting impatient because he knew what tunes were like. But the only things he could hear were the faint sounds of rain and running water. It gradually got quite dark. Snufkin took out his pipe but put it away again. He knew that the five bars must be somewhere in Moominvalley and that he wouldn't find them until he went back again.

There are millions of tunes that are easy to find and there will always be new ones. But Snufkin let them alone, they were summer songs which would do for just anybody. He crept into his tent and into his sleeping-bag and pulled it over his head. The faint whisper of rain and running water was still there and it had the same tender note of solitude and perfection. But what did the rain mean to him as long as he couldn't write a song about it?

CHAPTER 5

Hemulen

THE Hemulen woke up slowly and recognized himself and wished he had been someone he didn't know. He felt even tireder than when he went to bed, and here it was – another day which would go on until evening and then there would be another one and another one which would be the same as all days are when they are lived by a hemulen.

He crept under the bedcover and buried his nose in the pillow, then he shifted his stomach to the edge of the bed where the sheets were cool. He took possession of the whole bed with outstretched arms and legs, he was waiting for a nice dream that wouldn't come. He curled up and made himself small but it didn't help a bit. He tried being the hemulen that everybody liked, he tried being the hemulen that no one liked. But however hard he tried he remained a hemulen doing his best without anything really coming off. In the end he got up and pulled on his trousers.

The Hemulen didn't like getting dressed and undressed,

it gave him a feeling that the days passed without anything of importance happening. Even so, he spent the whole day arranging, organizing and directing things from morning till night! All around him there were people living slipshod and aimless lives, wherever he looked there was something to be put to rights and he worked his fingers to the bone trying to get them to see how they ought to live.

It's as though they don't want to live well, the Hemulen thought sadly as he brushed his teeth. He looked at the photograph of himself with his boat which had been taken when the boat was launched. It was a beautiful picture but it made him feel even sadder.

I ought to learn how to sail, the Hemulen thought. But I've never got enough time . . .

Suddenly the Hemulen thought that all he ever did was to move things from one place to another or talk about where they should be put, and in a moment of insight he wondered what would happen if he let things alone.

Actually, nothing, somebody else would look after everything, the Hemulen said to himself and put his toothbrush back in its glass. He was surprised and a little frightened by what he had said and a chill went down his spine as it did when the clock struck twelve on New Year's Eve, and he immediately thought but then I must go sailing . . . Then he felt really sick and went and sat down on the bed.

Now I don't understand anything, thought the poor old Hemulen. What on earth did I say anything like that for? There are certain things one shouldn't think about, one shouldn't go into things too deeply. He tried to find something pleasant to think about that would drive away his morning melancholy, he tried and tried and gradually a friendly and distant memory of summer came to him. The

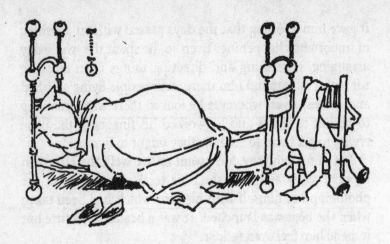

Hemulen remembered Moominvalley. It was a terribly long time since he had been there, but there was one thing he remembered quite clearly. It was the guest room facing south, and he recalled how nice it was to wake up there in the morning. The window was open and a gentle summer breeze stirred the white curtains, the window-catch rattled softly in the wind . . . And the fly that buzzed on the ceiling. And that there was no hurry to do anything. Morning coffee was waiting on the veranda, everything would arrange itself and go of its own accord.

There was a family there, too, but he didn't remember them very clearly, they pottered to and fro and went about their business in a friendly and vague sort of way — a family, in other words. Moominpappa he could remember a little more clearly, and perhaps Moominpappa's boat. And the jetty, too. But best of all he remembered what it felt like to wake up in the morning and feel happy.

The Hemulen got up, went to get his toothbrush and stuffed it in his pocket. He no longer felt sick, he felt like a completely new hemulen.

No one saw the Hemulen leave, without a suitcase, without an umbrella and without saying good-bye to a single one of his neighbours.

The Hemulen wasn't used to walking in the countryside. He lost his way several times, but that didn't make him feel either uneasy or angry.

I've never got lost before, he thought bravely. And I've never been wet-through before! He waved his arms about and felt like the man in the song who walked alone in the rain a thousand miles from home and was wild and free. The Hemulen felt so happy! And soon he would be drinking hot coffee on the veranda.

Less than a mile east of the valley the Hemulen came down to the river, looked thoughtfully at the dark running water and the thought occurred to him that life was like a river. Some people sailed on it slowly, some quickly, and some capsized. I'll tell that to Moominpappa, the Hemulen thought gravely. I think it must be a completely new thought. Just fancy, thoughts come easily today, and everything has become so straightforward. All you have to do is

to walk out of the door with your hat on at a jaunty angle! Perhaps I'll take the boat out. I'll sail out to sea. I can feel the firm pressure of the rudder on my paw ... The firm pressure of the rudder on my paw, the Hemulen repeated, and now he felt so happy that it almost hurt. He tightened his belt round his fat stomach and walked on along the river.

When the Hemulen got to the valley it was filled with a fine, drizzling rain. He walked straight into the garden and stopped, with a puzzled look on his face. Something wasn't right. Everything was the same but somehow not the same. A withered leaf floated down and landed on his nose.

How silly, the Hemulen exclaimed. It's not summer at all. It's autumn! In some way or another he had always thought of Moominvalley in summer. He went up to the house, stopped in front of the veranda steps and tried to yodel. He couldn't. Then he shouted: 'Hallo there, you inside! Put the coffee on!'

Nothing happened. The Hemulen shouted again and waited a while.

Now I'll play a trick on them, he thought. He pulled up his collar and dragged his hat down over his nose, then he found a rake by the water-butt and lifted it threateningly above his head. Then he yelled: 'Open in the name of the Law!'

He stood still and waited, shaking with laughter. The house was silent. It rained more heavily, falling and falling over the Hemulen as he waited, and nothing could be heard in the valley except the swish of falling rain.

CHAPTER 6

First Encounter

TOFT had never been in Moominvalley, but he didn't get lost. It was a very long way there and Toft's legs were short. Everywhere there were deep pools and swamps and great trees that had fallen down with age or been blown over by a storm. Their torn roots lifted huge lumps of earth into the air and underneath them pools of black water glistened. Toft walked round them, he walked round every single swamp and every single pool and didn't get lost once. He felt very happy because he knew exactly what he wanted. The forest smelt good, even better than the Hemulen's boat.

The Hemulen himself smelt of old paper and worry. Toft knew it. Once the Hemulen had stood outside his boat and sighed and tugged at the tarpaulin a bit and then gone away.

It wasn't raining at the moment but the forest was covered in mist and looked very beautiful, and it got thicker and thicker where the hills went down into Moominvalley, and little by little the pools became rivulets, more and more of them, and Toft walked between hundreds of streams and waterfalls, and all of them were going in the same direction as he was.

Moominvalley was very near now, he was there. He recognized the birch-trees because their trunks were paler than in any other valley. Everything light was lighter and everything dark was darker. Toft walked as quietly as he could and very slowly. He listened. Someone was chopping wood in the valley. It was Moominpappa chopping wood for the winter. Toft walked even more quietly, his paws hardly touching the mossy ground. The river came towards him, and there was the bridge and there was the road. Moominpappa had stopped chopping, and now there was only the sound of the river where all the rivulets and streams came together and went down to the sea.

I've arrived, Toft thought. He crossed the bridge and entered the garden and it was just as he had described it to himself, it couldn't possibly have been different. The trees

stood leafless in the November mist but for a moment they were all clothed in green, the little spots of sunlight danced in the grass and Toft could feel the sweet, comforting smell of lilac.

He ran all the way to the woodshed, but there a different smell came towards him, a smell of old paper and worry. The Hemulen was sitting on the steps of the woodshed with the axe in his lap. It had several nicks in the blade where he had struck nails. Toft stopped. That's the Hemulen, he thought. So that's what he looks like.

The Hemulen looked up. 'Hallo,' he said. 'I thought you were Moominpappa. Do you know where they've all gone to, eh?'

'No,' answered Toft.

'Their wood is full of nails,' the Hemulen explained and held up the axe. Old planks and bits of wood full of nails! It felt good to have someone to talk to. 'I came here just for fun,' the Hemulen continued. 'I just popped in to see old friends!' He laughed and put the axe away in the woodshed. 'Listen, Toft,' he said. 'Carry all this into the kitchen so that it can dry, and pile it up so that it faces first this way and then that way. Meanwhile I'll go and make some coffee. The kitchen is at the back of the house to the right.'

'I know,' answered Toft.

The Hemulen went towards the house and Toft began to gather the wood together. He could tell that the Hemulen wasn't used to chopping wood, but he had probably enjoyed himself. The wood smelt good.

*

The Hemulen carried the coffee-tray into the drawing-room and placed it on the oval mahogany table. 'The family have their coffee in the morning on the veranda usually,' he said. 'But coffee for visitors is served in the drawing-room, particularly when there's someone who has never been here before.'

The chairs were covered in dark red velvet, and there was a lace cloth on the back of each of them. Toft gazed timidly round the beautiful but awe-inspiring room. He didn't dare sit down, the furniture was much too grand. The tiled stove went right up to the ceiling and was painted with a pine-cone design, it had a damper-cord decorated with beads and shiny brass doors. The desk was also shiny and there was a gilded handle on every drawer.

'Well, aren't you going to sit down?' the Hemulen said.

Toft sat right on the edge of a chair and stared at the portrait hanging above the desk, which portrayed some-body with shaggy grey hair, close-set eyes and a tail. The nose was unusually large.

'That's their Ancestor,' the Hemulen explained. 'He's from the time when they lived behind stoves.'

Toft's glance moved to the staircase, which disappeared into the darkness of the attic floor. He shivered and said: 'Wouldn't it be warmer in the kitchen?'

'I think you're right,' the Hemulen said. 'It might be nicer in the kitchen.' He picked up the tray and they left the deserted drawing-room.

*

All day they didn't mention the family that had gone away. The Hemulen walked about the garden raking leaves and talking about anything that came into his head, and Toft followed on behind and collected the leaves in a basket and said very little.

At one point the Hemulen stood looking at Moominpappa's blue crystal ball. 'Garden ornaments,' he said. 'When I was young they used to be silver-plated,' and then he went on raking.

Toft didn't look at the crystal ball. He didn't want to look at it until he was alone. The crystal ball was the focal point of the whole valley and it always mirrored those who lived there. If there was anything left of the Moomin family then one ought to be able to see them in the deep-blue crystal ball.

*

At dusk the Hemulen went into the drawing-room and wound up Moominpappa's grandfather clock. It started off by striking like something possessed, rapidly and unevenly, and then it began to work. The clock was ticking again, steadily and quite calmly, and the drawing-room had come to life again. The Hemulen went up to the barometer, a large dark mahogany barometer covered with ornamental work, tapped it and saw that it said: Unsettled. After that he went into the kitchen and said: 'Things are getting organized now! We can have another fire and a little more coffee, what?' He lit the kitchen lamp and found some cinnamon biscuits in the cupboard.

'These are real ship's biscuits,' he explained. 'They remind me of my boat. Eat, Toft! You're too thin.'

'Thank you very much,' said Toft.

The Hemulen was in high spirits. He leant over the kitchen table and said: 'My sailing boat is clinker-built. Is there anything to compare with getting a boat into the water when spring comes?'

Toft dunked his biscuit in his coffee and said nothing.

'You wait and wait,' said the Hemulen, 'and at last you set sail and you're off.'

Toft looked up at the Hemulen from under his fringe. Finally all he said was: 'Yes.'

The Hemulen was suddenly gripped by a feeling of loneliness, it was too quiet in the house. He said: 'It isn't always that one has time to do just what one wants. Did you know them?'

'Yes, Moominmamma,' Toft answered. 'The others are a little hazy in my mind.'

'They are in mine, too,' the Hemulen exclaimed, relieved that Toft had at last said something. 'I never looked at them very closely, they were just there, you know . . .' He fumbled for words, and went on tentatively: 'They were just like things that are always around, if you see what I mean . . . Like trees, eh? . . . or . . . things.'

Toft retired into himself again. After a while the Hemulen got up and said: 'Perhaps it's about time to go to bed. Tomorrow's another day.' He hesitated. The beautiful image of the summer and the guest room facing south had vanished, now he could only see the staircase leading up to the dark attic floor with empty rooms. He decided to sleep in the kitchen.

'I'm going outside for a while,' Toft muttered.

He shut the door behind him and stood on the kitchen steps. It was as black as jet outside. He waited until his eyes got used to the dark and then walked slowly through the garden. Something blue and radiant appeared out of the night, he'd reached the crystal ball. He looked right into it, it was as deep as the sea and was flooded with a tremendous swell. Toft looked deeper and deeper and waited patiently. At last, deep down inside the ball, he could see a faint point of light. It shone and then disappeared, shone and disappeared at regular intervals, like a lighthouse.

What a long way away they are, Toft thought. He felt the cold creeping up his legs but he stayed where he was staring at the light which came and went, so faint that one could only just see it. He felt as though they had deceived him somehow.

*

The Hemulen stood in the kitchen holding the lamp in his paw and thinking what an impossible and unpleasant task it was hunting for a mattress, finding a place to put it, and then to undress and confess that yet another day had become yet another night. How did things get like this, he thought, quite dumbfounded. I have felt so happy all day. What was it that was so simple?

While the Hemulen stood there wondering, the veranda door opened and someone came into the drawing-room and knocked over a chair.

'What are you doing in there?' the Hemulen asked.

No one answered. The Hemulen lifted up the lamp and shouted: 'Who's there?!'

A very old voice answered mysteriously: 'That I have no intention of telling you!'

CHAPTER 7

Grandpa-Grumble

HE was frightfully old and forgot things very easily. One dark autumn morning he woke up and had forgotten what his name was. It's a little sad when you forget other people's names but it's lovely to be able to completely forget your own.

He didn't bother about getting up, and the whole day he let pictures and thoughts come and go in his mind just as they pleased; he slept sometimes and woke up again still not knowing who he was. It was a peaceful and very exciting day.

Towards evening he tried to find a name for himself so that he would be able to get up. Crumby-Mumble? Grindle-Fumble? Grandpa-Grumble? Gramble-Fimble? Mamble . . . ?

There are so many people you're introduced to who immediately lose their names. They always come on Sundays. They shout polite questions because they can never learn that you're not deaf. They try to talk as simply as possible so that you'll understand what it is they're on about. They say good night and go home and play and dance and sing until the next morning. They're all relations of yours.

I am Grandpa-Grumble, he whispered solemnly. I shall get up now and forget all the families in the world.

Grandpa-Grumble sat by his window most of the night and looked out into the darkness, he was full of expectation. Someone passed his house and went straight into the forest. A lighted window was reflected in the water on the other side of the bay. Perhaps there was a party going on and perhaps there wasn't. The night passed quietly while Grandpa-Grumble waited to know what he wanted to do.

There came a moment in the darkness of early dawn when he knew that he wanted to go to a valley where he had once been a very long time ago. It was just possible that he had only heard about this valley, or perhaps he had read about it, but it made no difference really. The most important thing was the brook that ran through the valley. Or perhaps it was a river? But certainly not a stream. Grandpa-Grumble decided that it was a brook, for he liked brooks much more than streams. A clear, flowing brook, with him sitting on the bridge and dangling his legs as he watched the little fish swimming round each other. No one to ask him whether he ought to go to bed. No one to ask him how he was and then start talking about other things without giving him time to work out whether he felt well or not. There was a place there, too, where one could play and sing all night, and Grandpa-Grumble would be the last to go home at dawn.

Grandpa-Grumble didn't leave straightaway. He had learnt the importance of putting off the thing you're longing for and he knew that an excursion into the unknown must be prepared with the proper consideration.

For several days he wandered in the hills surrounding the long, dark bay, sinking deeper and deeper into forgetfulness, and he began to feel that the valley was getting nearer and nearer.

The last red and yellow leaves fell off the trees and gathered round his feet as he walked (Grandpa-Grumble still had very good legs) and from time to time he stopped and picked up a leaf with his stick and said to himself: that's maple. I shan't forget that. He knew perfectly well what he wanted to remember.

It was incredible how much he succeeded in forgetting during those few days. Every morning he woke up with the same secretive expectation, and immediately started about the business of forgetting in order to make the valley come nearer. No one disturbed him, no one told him who he was.

Grandpa-Grumble found a basket under his bed and packed it with all his medicines and the little bottle of brandy for his stomach. He made six sandwiches and dug out his umbrella. He was getting ready to escape, he was running away from home.

Over the years many things had accumulated on his floor. There are so many things you never bother to pick up, and so many reasons for not picking them up. These objects lay scattered all over the place like so many islands, an archipelago of lost and unnecessary things. Out of habit he stepped over them and round them, they gave his daily walks round the room a certain excitement and at the same time a feeling of repetition and permanence. Grandpa-Grumble decided that they weren't needed any longer. He took a broom and made a storm sweep through the room.

Everything, scraps of food, lost slippers, bits of fluff, pills that had rolled into corners, forgotten shopping-lists, spoons and forks and buttons and unopened letters, he brushed them all into a heap. From this great heap he picked out eight pairs of spectacles and put them in his basket: I shall be looking at quite new things, he thought.

The valley was now quite close, just around the corner, and he had a feeling that it wasn't even Sunday yet.

On Friday or Saturday Grandpa-Grumble left his house, and naturally he couldn't help writing a farewell note. 'I'm going away now and I feel fine,' he wrote. 'I've heard everything you've said for a hundred years because I'm not deaf at all and I know you have parties on the sly all the time.' No signature.

Then Grandpa-Grumble put on his dressing-gown and his gaiters, he picked up his little basket, opened his door and closed it behind him, shutting in a hundred old years. Strengthened by his determination and his new name he headed due north towards the Happy Valley and nobody in the bay knew that he had gone. Red and yellow leaves danced round his head and from far away in the hills came another autumn downpour to wash away the last of everything he didn't want to remember.

CHAPTER 8

Lady in a Muddle

FILLYJONK'S visit to Moominvalley was postponed a little because she couldn't decide about the moth-balls. Putting moth-balls in everything is a big operation, with airing and brushing and all that, not to mention the wardrobes themselves, which had to be scrubbed with soda and soap. But as soon as Fillyjonk touched a broom or a duster she felt dizzy, and a giddy feeling of fear started in her stomach and got stuck in her throat. She couldn't do any cleaning, it was no good. Not after that business of washing the window.

This won't do, poor Fillyjonk thought. The moths will eat up everything I possess!

She had no idea how long her visit would last. If she didn't enjoy it the whole thing might be over in a couple of days. But if she was enjoying herself it might last a month. And if it was a month, her clothes might be full of moths and carpet-beetles when she got home. With horror she imagined their little jaws eating through her clothes, her carpets – and their wicked delight when they found her feather-boa!

In the end Fillyjonk was so tired and overcome with not being able to make up her mind that she flung her feather-boa round her neck, locked the house and started off.

Moominvalley wasn't far from her house but when she arrived her suitcase felt as heavy as lead and her boots hurt her. She went up on the veranda and knocked on the door, waited a little and then went into the drawing-room.

Fillyjonk saw immediately that no one had cleaned up there for a long time. She took off one of her cotton gloves and ran her finger along the edge of the stove, making a white line in the grey dust. It can't be true, she whispered, and a shudder of agitation went through her. To stop cleaning, and of your own free will, too . . . She put her suitcase down and went over to the window. It was dirty as well, the rain had left long melancholy streaks all over the pane. Only when Fillyjonk noticed that the curtains had been taken down did she understand that the family wasn't at home at all. She saw that the chandelier had been wrapped in muslin. And all of a sudden the chilly smell of the deserted house enveloped her and she felt utterly deceived. She opened her suitcase and took out the china vase, the present for Moominmamma, and put it on the table. It stood there as a silent reproach. It was terribly quiet everywhere.

Suddenly Fillyjonk dashed upstairs. It was even chillier there, the kind of stagnant cold you find in a summer-house that has been closed up for the winter. She opened one door after another, all the rooms were empty and in semi-darkness with the blinds down. She became more and more uneasy and began to open the wardrobes, tried to open the clothes-cupboard but it was locked, and suddenly she went quite crazy and hammered on the cupboard door with

47

both paws, then she rushed up to the box-room and pulled the door open.

There inside sat Toft, staring at her. He had a big book in his lap and looked frightened.

'Where are they? Where are they?' shouted Fillyjonk.

Toft dropped his book and crept against the wall, but when he caught the smell of this strange, excited fillyjonk he knew that she wasn't dangerous. She smelt of fear. He said: 'I don't know.'

'But I've come to see them!' Fillyjonk exclaimed. 'I have

a present with me. A very fine vase. They can't have moved
away just like that without saying a word!'

Toft just shook his head and went on staring at her.
Then Fillyjonk shut the door behind her and went away.

Toft crept back into the roach-net that lay rolled up on
the floor and made a fresh comfortable hollow for himself
and went on reading. It was a very big book which had no
beginning and no end and the pages were all faded and had
been nibbled by rats at the edges. Toft wasn't used to
reading and it took him a long time to spell his way through
every line. All the time he was hoping that the book would
explain to him why the family had gone away and where
they all were. But the book was about quite different
things, curious beasts and murky landscapes and nothing
had a name that he recognized. Toft had never known
before that deep down at the bottom of the sea lived

Radiolaria and the very last Nummulites. One of the Nummulites wasn't like his relatives, there was something of Noctiluca, about him, and little by little he was like nothing except himself. He was evidently very tiny and became even tinier when he was frightened.

'It is impossible for us to express sufficient amazement,' read Toft, 'at this rare variant of the Protozoa group. The reason for its peculiar development naturally evades all possibility of well-founded judgement, but we have grounds for conjecturing that an electrical charge was a crucial necessity of life for it. The occurrence of electrical storms at that period was exceptionally abundant, the post-glacial mountain chains described above being subjected to the unceasing turbulence of these violent electrical storms, and the adjacent ocean became charged with electricity.'

Toft let the book fall. He didn't really understand what it was all about and the sentences were so long. But he thought all the strange words were beautiful, and he had never had a book of his own before. He hid it under the roach-net and lay still, thinking. A little bat was hanging from the broken skylight, sleeping upside down.

He heard Fillyjonk's shrill voice in the garden, she had found the Hemulen.

Toft felt very sleepy. He tried to describe the Happy Family, but he couldn't. Then he told himself all about the solitary creature instead, the little Nummulite who had something of Noctiluca about him and liked electricity.

CHAPTER 9
Mymble

MYMBLE was walking through the forest and she thought: it's nice being a mymble. I feel absolutely splendid from top to toe.

She liked her long legs and her red boots. On top of her head sat her haughty mymble hair-do, glossy and tight and a soft reddish-yellow like a little onion. She went through swamps and up hills and through the deep hollows that the rain had transformed into under-water landscapes, she walked quickly and sometimes she broke into a run just to feel how light and thin she was.

Mymble had got an urge to go and see her little sister, Little My, whom the Moomin family had adopted some time ago. She imagined that Little My was just as down-to-earth and bad-tempered as ever and that she could still squeeze into a sewing-basket.

When Mymble arrived Grandpa-Grumble was sitting on the bridge fishing with a home-made contraption. He was wearing his dressing-gown, gaiters and hat, and holding an umbrella. Mymble had never seen him close to, and she scrutinized him carefully and with a certain curiosity. He was surprisingly small.

'I know who you are all right,' he said. 'And I am Grandpa-Grumble and nobody else! And I know you have parties on the sly because I can see the lights on in your windows all night!'

'If you believe that, you'd believe anything,' Mymble answered unconcerned. 'Have you seen Little My?'

Grandpa-Grumble pulled his contraption out of the water. It was empty.

'Where's Little My?' Mymble asked.

'Don't shout!' Grandpa-Grumble yelled. 'There's nothing wrong with my ears, and the fish may get scared and swim away!'

'They did that long ago,' said Mymble, and ran off. Grandpa-Grumble sneezed and crept further in under his umbrella. His brook had always been full of fish. He looked down into the brown water rushing under the bridge in a glistening swollen mass, carrying with it thousands of floating, half-drowned objects which sped past and disappeared, all the time passing and disappearing . . . Grandpa-Grumble's eyes started to ache and he shut them in order to be able to see his own brook again, a clear brook with a sandy bottom and full of darting shiny fish . . .

There's something wrong here, he thought anxiously. The bridge is all right, it's the right one. But I'm what's quite new . . . His thoughts drifted away and he fell asleep.

*

Fillyjonk sat on the veranda with blankets over her legs and looking as though she owned the whole valley and wasn't very pleased about it.

'Hallo,' said Mymble. She could see at once that the house was empty.

'Good morning,' Fillyjonk replied with the chilly charm she used for mymbles. 'They've all gone away. Without a word. One should feel grateful that the door wasn't locked!'

'They never lock their doors,' Mymble said.

'Yes they do,' Fillyjonk whispered and leant forward confidentially. 'They have locked doors. The clothes-cupboard upstairs is locked! Of course, that's where they keep their valuables, things they're afraid of losing!'

Mymble looked at Fillyjonk, her anxious eyes and her hair all in tight curls with a hair-grip in each and her feather-boa. Fillyjonk hadn't changed. The Hemulen came up the garden-path, he was raking leaves into a basket.

'Hallo,' said the Hemulen. 'So you're here too, are you?'

'Who's that?' Mymble asked.

'I brought a present with me,' Fillyjonk said behind her.

'Toft,' the Hemulen explained, 'he's helping me a bit in the garden.'

'A very fine china vase for Moominmamma! 'said Fillyjonk shrilly.

'Really,' said Mymble. 'And you're raking leaves.'

'I'm making the place look nice,' the Hemulen added.

Suddenly Fillyjonk shouted: 'You mustn't touch old leaves! They're dangerous! They're full of putrefaction!' She dashed to the front of the veranda with the blankets trailing behind her. 'Bacteria!' she screamed. 'Worms! Maggots! Creepy-crawlies! Don't touch them!'

The Hemulen went on raking. He screwed up his stubborn, innocent face and repeated loudly: 'I'm making the place look nice, for Moominpappa.'

'I know what I'm talking about,' said Fillyjonk menacingly, and came closer. Mymble watched them. Old leaves? she thought. People are odd . . . She went into the house and up to the attic. It was very cold there. The guest room facing south was just the same as it had always been, the white washstand, the faded picture of a storm ages ago, the blue eiderdown. The water-jug was empty and there was a dead spider at the bottom of it. Fillyjonk's suitcase was in the middle of the room and there was a pink nightdress lying on the bed.

Mymble took the suitcase and the nightdress into the guest room facing north and shut the door. The guest room facing south was hers, just as certainly as there was an old comb of hers underneath the lace doiley on the washstand. She lifted the doiley and the comb was there. Mymble sat down by the window, undid her lovely long hair and began to comb it. Down below, the morning quarrel continued noiselessly outside the closed windows.

Mymble combed and combed. Her hair crackled with small electric sparks and became glossier and glossier. She stared out of the window absent-mindedly at the garden, which the autumn had changed and turned into a strange and deserted landscape. The trees were like grey stage decorations, screens standing one behind the other in the wet mist, all quite bare. The noiseless quarrel in front of the veranda continued. They were waving their paws about, running this way and that and looking as unreal as the trees. Except Toft, he was standing quite still, staring at the ground.

*

A broad shadow came down the valley, more rain was coming. And there was Snufkin walking over the bridge. It must be him because no one else wore such green clothes. He stopped at the lilac-bushes and looked. Then he came closer, but now he was walking differently, much more slowly. Mymble opened the window.

The Hemulen flung the rake away. 'Huh! Organize indeed!' he said.

Fillyjonk said into the air: 'It was different in Moomin-mamma's day.'

Toft stood looking at her boots, he could see that they were too tight. The rain had come. The last sorrowful leaf relinquished its hold and floated down to the veranda, the rain got heavier and heavier.

'Hallo,' said Snufkin.

They looked at each other.

'It seems to be raining,' said Fillyjonk nervously. 'No one is at home.'

The Hemulen said: 'So nice that you're here.'

Snufkin made a vague gesture, tentatively, and crept in under the shadow of his hat. He turned round and went back to the river. The Hemulen and Fillyjonk followed him. They stood a little way away and waited while he put up his tent next to the bridge, and they watched him creep inside.

'It's nice that you're here,' the Hemulen said again.

They stayed there for a while and waited in the rain.

'He's gone to sleep,' the Hemulen whispered. 'He's tired.'

Mymble saw them coming back to the house. She shut the window and carefully put her hair up in a beautiful little tight knot.

There's nothing as lovely as being comfortable and nothing is so simple. Mymble didn't feel sorry for those people she met and then forgot, and she tried not to get mixed up in what they were doing. She regarded them and their mess with amused surprise.

The eiderdown was blue. Moominmamma had collected the down for six years and now the eiderdown lay in the guest room facing south inside its cover of crotcheted lace waiting for someone to be comfortable. Mymble decided to have a hot-water bottle at her feet, she knew where they were kept in this house. She would wash her hair in rain-water every fifth day. She would take a little nap at dusk. In the evening the kitchen would be warm from the cooking.

You can lie on a bridge and watch the water flowing past. Or run, or wade through a swamp in your red boots. Or roll yourself up and listen to the rain falling on the roof. It's very easy to enjoy yourself.

The November day moved slowly towards twilight. Mymble crept in under the eiderdown, stretched her long legs until they cracked and curled her toes round the hot-water bottle. It was raining outside. In a couple of hours she would feel hungry enough to eat Fillyjonk's dinner and perhaps she would feel like talking. But at the moment she didn't need to do anything except sink down in the warmth, the whole world was a single great big eiderdown which encircled a mymble and everything else was outside.

Mymble never dreamed, she slept when she felt like it and woke up when there was anything to make it worthwhile waking up.

CHAPTER 10

Late That Night

It was dark in the tent. Snufkin crept out of his sleeping-bag, the five bars had come no nearer. Not a sign of any music. Outside it was very quiet, the rain had stopped. He decided to fry some pork and went to the woodshed to get fuel.

When the fire was alight the Hemulen and Fillyjonk came down to the tent again and stood there watching without saying anything.

'Have you had dinner?' Snufkin asked.

'We can't,' the Hemulen answered. 'We can't agree about who's going to do the washing-up.'

'Toft,' said Fillyjonk.

'No, not Toft,' the Hemulen said. 'He's helping me in the garden. Fillyjonk and Mymble ought to keep house for us all, the womenfolk should do these things, eh? Don't you think I'm right? I can make the coffee and see to it that everybody has a nice time. And Grandpa-Grumble is so old, I'll let him please himself what he does.'

'Why do hemulens have to organize things for other people all the time!' Fillyjonk exclaimed.

They both looked at Snufkin anxiously and expectantly.

Washing-up, he thought. They don't know a thing about it. What is washing-up? Tossing a plate into the stream, rinsing one's paws, throwing away a green leaf, it's nothing at all. What are they talking about?

'Isn't it true that hemulens want to organize things the whole time?' Fillyjonk asked. 'This is important.'

Snufkin got up, he was a little scared of both of them. He tried to think of something to say, but he couldn't find an explanation that seemed fair.

Suddenly the Hemulen shouted: 'I won't organize a thing! I want to live in a tent and be independent!' He tore open the tent door and crept inside, filling the whole tent. 'You see what I mean,' Fillyjonk whispered. She waited for a moment or two and then went away.

Snufkin lifted the frying-pan off the fire, the pork was quite black. He filled his pipe. After a while he asked cautiously: 'Are you used to sleeping in a tent?'

The Hemulen answered gloomily: 'Living in the wilds is the best thing I know.'

It was now quite dark. Up at the house two windows were lit and the light was just as steady and just as soft as it always used to be in the evenings.

*

In the guest room facing north Fillyjonk lay with the blanket pulled up round her nose and her head full of curlers which hurt her neck. She lay counting knots in the ceiling and she was hungry.

All the time, right from the beginning, Fillyjonk had thought that she would be the one to prepare the food. She loved arranging small jars and bags on the shelves, she thought it was fun to work out new ways of doing up left-overs in puddings and rissoles so that nobody could recognize them. She loved doing the cooking as economically as possible, and knowing that not a single drop of semolina had been wasted.

The family's great gong hung on the veranda. Fillyjonk had always longed to be the one who announced dinner, making the sonorous brass resound, dong dong, through the valley until everybody came running and shouting: 'Food! food! What have you got for us today? We're so hungry!'

Tears came into Fillyjonk's eyes. The Hemulen had spoilt everything for her. She would willingly have done the washing-up, provided it had been her own idea. Fillyjonk should look after the housekeeping because that's what womenfolk do! Huh! And with Mymble, what's more!

Fillyjonk put out the light so that it wouldn't burn quite unnecessarily and pulled the blanket over her head. The stairs squeaked. A very, very faint rattling sound came from the drawing-room. Somewhere in the empty house someone shut a door. How can there be so many sounds in an empty house, Fillyjonk thought. Then she remembered that the house was full of people. But somehow she still thought it was empty.

*

Grandpa-Grumble lay on the drawing-room sofa with his nose buried in the best velvet cushion and heard somebody creeping into the kitchen. There was a very faint sound of clinking glass. He sat up in the dark and pricked up his ears and thought: they're having a party.

Now it was quite quiet again. Grandpa-Grumble went across the cold floor and crept up to the kitchen door. The kitchen was dark, too, but a ray of light shone from under the pantry door.

Aha, he thought. They've hidden themselves in the pantry. He jerked open the door, and there sat Mymble eating pickled gherkins, with two candles burning on the shelf beside her.

'So you had the same idea,' she said. 'There are the pickled gherkins and there are the cinnamon biscuits. Those are mustard pickles, you'd better not eat them, they're too strong for you.'

Grandpa-Grumble immediately took the jar of pickles and started eating. He didn't think they were much good, but he went on eating them all the same.

After a while Mymble said: 'They'll upset your stomach. You'll explode and drop dead on the spot.'

'One doesn't die on holiday,' Grandpa-Grumble said cheerfully. 'What's that in the soup tureen?'

'Spruce-needles,' Mymble answered. 'They fill their stomachs with them before they hibernate.' She lifted the lid: 'The Ancestor seems to have stuffed most of them.'

'What Ancestor?' Grandpa-Grumble asked, surreptitiously changing over to gherkins.

'He's in the stove,' Mymble explained. 'He's three hundred years old and is hibernating just now.'

Grandpa-Grumble said nothing. He couldn't quite decide whether he felt pleased or offended that there was someone who was even older than himself. His interest was aroused and he made up his mind to wake up the Ancestor and make his acquaintance.

'Listen,' Mymble said, 'it's not worth trying to wake him up. He won't wake up till April. You've got through half that jar of gherkins.'

Grandpa-Grumble snorted and screwed up his face, stuffed his pockets with gherkins and cinnamon biscuits, took one of the candles and shuffled back into the drawing-room. He put the candle on the floor in front of the stove and opened the doors. There was nothing but darkness inside. He lifted the candle into the stove and looked again. All there was was a piece of paper and a little soot that had fallen down the chimney.

'Are you there?' he called. 'Wake up! I want to see what you look like!' But the Ancestor didn't answer; he was hibernating with his stomach full of spruce-needles.

Grandpa-Grumble picked up the piece of paper and saw that it was a letter. He sat on the floor and tried to remember where he had left his glasses. But he couldn't. Then he hid the letter in a safe place, blew out the candle and crept in among the cushions again.

I wonder whether the Ancestor is allowed to join in when they have a party, he thought gloomily. Never mind. I've had a very enjoyable day. A day that's been my very own.

*

Toft lay in the box-room reading his book. The light at his side made a little circle of safety in this strange, great house.

'As we intimated earlier,' Toft read, 'this curious species gathered its energy from the electrical charges which regularly accumulated in these elongated valleys and illuminated the night with their white and violet light. We can picture to ourselves the last of this virtually extinct species of Nummulites gradually rising to the surface, struggling towards the boundless swamps of the rain-drenched forests where the lightning was reflected in the bubbles rising from the ooze, and finally abandoning his original element.'

He must have been really lonely, Toft thought. He wasn't like any of the others and his family didn't bother about him, so he left. I wonder where he is now and whether I shall ever be able to meet him. Perhaps he'll show himself if I can describe him clearly enough.

Toft said: end of the chapter, and put out the light.

CHAPTER II

Next Morning

IN the long, vague dawn as the November night changed to morning, the fog moved in from the sea. It rolled up the hillsides and slid down into the valleys on the other side and filled every corner of them. Snufkin had determined that he would wake up early in order to have an hour or two to himself. His fire had burnt out long ago but he didn't feel cold. He had that simple but rare ability to retain his own warmth, he gathered it all round him and lay very still and took care not to dream.

The fog had brought complete silence with it, the valley was quite motionless.

Snufkin woke up as quickly as an animal, wide awake. The five bars had come a little nearer.

Good, he thought. A cup of coffee and I'll get them. (He ought to have skipped the coffee.)

The morning fire picked up and began to burn. Snufkin filled the coffee-pot with water from the river and put it on the fire, took a step backwards and tumbled over the Hemulen's rake. With a terrible clatter his saucepan rolled down the river bank, and the Hemulen stuck his nose out of the tent and said: 'Hallo!'

'Hallo!' said Snufkin.

The Hemulen crawled up to the fire with the sleeping-bag over his head, he was cold and sleepy but quite determined to be amiable. 'Life in the wilds!' he said.

Snufkin saw to the coffee.

'Just think,' the Hemulen continued, 'being able to hear all the mysterious sounds of the night from inside a real tent! I'm sure you've got something for a stiff neck, haven't you?'

'No,' said Snufkin. 'Do you want sugar or not?'

'Sugar, yes, four lumps preferably.' His front was now getting warm and the small of his back didn't ache so much any more. The coffee was very hot.

'What's so nice about you,' said the Hemulen confidentially, 'is that you are so little. You must be terribly clever because you don't say anything. It makes me want to talk about my boat.'

The fog had lifted a little, quite quietly, and the black wet ground began to appear around them and round the Hemulen's big boots, but his head was still in the fog. Everything was almost as usual, except his neck. The coffee warmed his stomach and suddenly he felt gay and without a care in the world: 'You know what,' he said, 'you and I understand each other. Moominpappa's boat is down by the bathing-hut. That's where it is, isn't it?'

And they remembered the jetty, narrow and solitary, resting shakily on blackening piles and the bathing-hut at the end of it with its pointed roof and red and green window-panes and the steep steps leading down into the water.

'I'm not sure that the boat is still there,' said Snufkin, putting his mug down. He thought: they've sailed away. I don't feel like talking about them with this hemulen. But the Hemulen leant forward and said gravely: 'We must go and have a look. Just you and me, it'll feel better that way.'

They went off into the fog, which lifted and began to drift out of the way. In the forest it was an endless white ceiling held up by the black pillars of the tree-trunks, a tall, solemn landscape created for silence. The Hemulen thought about his boat but said nothing. He followed Snufkin all the way down to the sea and at last everything had become uncomplicated and meaningful again.

The bathing-hut jetty was the same as ever. The sailing-boat wasn't there. The duckboards and the fish-basket lay above the high-water line and they had pulled the little dinghy right up to the trees. The fog drifted away over the water and everything was soft and grey, the beach, the air, and the silence.

'You know how I feel,' the Hemulen burst out, 'I feel quite – quite strange! My neck's not stiff any longer.' He had a sudden desire to confide and to tell Snufkin about his efforts to arrange everything so that other people could enjoy themselves, but he was too shy and couldn't find the words he needed. Snufkin walked on. A dark bank of every-thing that storm and high-water had thrown up, discarded things, forgotten things, all jumbled up under seaweed and reeds, heavy and blackened with water, covered the beach as far as the eye could see. The splintered timbers were full of old nails and bent cramp-irons. The sea had devoured the beach right up to the first trees, and there was seaweed hanging in their branches.

'It's been blowing very hard,' said Snufkin.

'I'm trying so terribly hard,' the Hemulen exclaimed behind him. 'I want to so awfully much.'

Snufkin made his usual vague noise which meant that he

had heard but had nothing to add. He walked along the bathing-hut jetty. The sandy bottom underneath the jetty was covered with a brown mass that rocked gently with the movement of the water, it was seaweed which the storm had torn to little pieces. The fog had gone, and there wasn't an emptier beach in the whole world.

'You understand,' the Hemulen said.

Snufkin bit his pipe and stared down into the water. 'Yes, yes,' he said. And after a while: 'I think that all small boats should be clinker-built.'

'I think so, too,' the Hemulen agreed. 'My boat is clinker-built. It's absolutely the nicest thing for small boats. And it should be tarred and not varnished, shouldn't it? I tar my boat every spring before I go out sailing. Listen. Can you help me with one thing? It's the sail. I can't decide whether I should have a white one or a red one. White's always a good colour, sort of classical? But then I happened to think of red, it's so daring in a way? What do you think? Do you think it would look a bit provocative?'

'No, I don't think so,' Snufkin answered. 'Have the red one.' He felt sleepy and he didn't want to do anything except crawl into his tent and shut himself in.

All the way back the Hemulen talked about his boat. 'It's strange,' he said, 'I feel such kinship with everybody who likes boats. Moominpappa, for example. One fine day he hoists sail and is off, just like that. Completely free. Sometimes, you know, sometimes I think that Moominpappa and I are alike. Only a little of course, but even so . . .'

Snufkin made his vague noise.

'Yes, it's true,' said the Hemulen quietly. 'And don't you think there's something significant in the fact that his boat is called the *Adventure*?'

They separated at the tent.

'It's been a wonderful morning,' the Hemulen said. 'Thanks a lot for letting me talk.'

Snufkin shut himself in. His tent was that green summery colour that makes one think the sun is shining outside.

*

When the Hemulen approached the house the morning was over. Now the day was beginning for the others, they didn't know anything about what he'd been given. Fillyjonk opened her window to air the room.

'Good morning!' the Hemulen called. 'I slept in the tent! I heard all the noises of the night!'

'What noises?' Fillyjonk asked sourly, and secured the window catch.

'The noises of the night,' the Hemulen repeated. 'I mean the noises one can hear in the night.'

'Really,' said Fillyjonk.

She didn't like windows, they're unsafe, you never know with windows, they blow open, they slam shut . . . It was colder in the guest room facing north than it was outside. She sat down in front of the mirror, shivered a little and took the curlers out of her hair and thought that she always lived facing north, even in her own house, just because everything is the wrong way round for a fillyjonk. Her hair hadn't dried properly, no wonder in a damp room like this, the curls fell out like straightened pokers, everything was wrong, everything, even her morning hair-do which was so important to her, and with Mymble in the house, too. The house was damp and musty and dusty and ought to be aired, a cross-draught through all the rooms and masses of warm water and a marvellous, colossal, thorough spring-cleaning . . .

Hardly had Fillyjonk thought of spring-cleaning when a wave of dizziness and nausea overcame her and for one terrifying moment she was hanging over the abyss. She knew: I shall never again be able to clean. How can I go on living if I can neither clean or prepare food? There's nothing else worth doing.

Fillyjonk went very slowly downstairs. The others were sitting on the veranda drinking coffee. Fillyjonk looked at them. She looked at Grandpa-Grumble's buckled hat and

Toft's tousled head, the Hemulen's solid neck, which was a little red from the chill morning air, there they all sat and Mymble's hair was, oh dear, so beautiful – and suddenly Fillyjonk was overcome by a great tiredness and she thought: they don't like me at all.

She stood in the middle of the drawing-room and looked around. The Hemulen had wound up the clock, he had tapped the barometer. The furniture was all in place and everything that had ever happened in the room was shut away and out of sight and didn't want to have anything to do with her.

Suddenly, quickly, Fillyjonk went to fetch some wood from the kitchen. She wanted to make a big fire in the stove to warm up the desolate house and all those who were attempting to live in it.

*

'Listen you in there, whatever your name is,' shouted Grandpa-Grumble outside the tent. 'I've saved the Ancestor! My friend the Ancestor! She had forgotten that he lives in the stove, how could she! And now she's lying on her bed crying.'

'Who?' Snufkin asked.

'The one who wears the feather-boa, of course,' exclaimed Grandpa-Grumble. 'Isn't it awful?!'

'She's calming herself down,' Snufkin muttered from inside the tent.

Grandpa-Grumble was taken aback, he was very disappointed. He thumped his stick on the ground and said many disgraceful things to himself, and then went down to the bridge, where Mymble was sitting combing her hair.

'Did you see how I saved the Ancestor?' he asked severely. 'One second more and he would have burnt up.'

73

'But he wasn't,' said Mymble.

Grandpa-Grumble explained to Mymble: 'None of you understands when something big happens nowadays. You all have the wrong feelings. Perhaps you don't even admire me.' He pulled up his fishing contraption. It was empty.

'It's in the spring that there are fish in this river,' said Mymble.

'It isn't a river, it's a brook,' he shouted. 'It's my brook and it's full of fish!'

'Now listen, Grandpa-Grumble,' said Mymble calmly. 'It's neither a river nor a brook. It's a stream. But if the Moomin family call it a river, it's a river. I'm the only one who can see that it's a stream. Why do you want to make such a fuss about things that don't exist and things that haven't happened?'

'To make things more fun,' Grandpa-Grumble replied.

Mymble combed and combed and the comb rustled like water on a sandy beach, wave after wave, lazily and untroubled.

Grandpa-Grumble stood up and said with great dignity: 'If you do see this as a stream, do you have to mention it? Horrid child, why do you want to make me feel unhappy?'

Mymble stopped combing her hair, she was very surprised. 'I like you,' she said, 'I don't want to make you feel unhappy.'

'That's good,' said Grandpa-Grumble. 'But you must stop telling me about the way things are and let me go on believing in nice things.'

'I'll try,' Mymble said.

Grandpa-Grumble was very upset. He stamped off to the tent and shouted: 'You inside there! Is this a brook or is it a river or is it a stream? Are there any fish in it or not? Why is nothing like it used to be? And when are you coming out to take an interest in things?'

'Soon,' Snufkin answered peevishly. He listened anxiously, but Grandpa-Grumble didn't say anything else.

I must go and join them, Snufkin thought. This is no good. Whatever did I come back here for? What have I got to do with them? They know nothing about music. He rolled over on his back, he turned on his stomach, he buried his nose in the sleeping-bag. But whatever he did, there they were in his tent, all the time, the Hemulen's immobile eyes, and Fillyjonk lying weeping on her bed, and Toft who just kept quiet and stared at the ground and old Grandpa-Grumble all confused ... they were everywhere, right inside his head, and, what's more, the tent smelt of the Hemulen. I must go outside, Snufkin thought. Thinking about them is worse than being with them. And how different they are from the Moomin family. They were a nuisance, too, they wanted to talk. They were all over the place. But with them you could at least be on your own. How *did* they behave, actually? Snufkin wondered in surprise. How is it possible that I could have been with them all those long summers without ever noticing that they let me be alone?

CHAPTER 12

Thunder and Lightning

TOFT read very slowly and carefully: 'No words can describe the period of confusion that must have followed upon the non-appearance of the electricity. We have reason to suppose that this Nummulite, this isolated phenomenon which, despite everything, can still be assigned to the Protozoa group, was retarded in his development and underwent a period of stunted growth. The ability to phosphoresce ceased and the unfortunate creature led a life of concealment in the cracks and deep hollows which provided a temporary shelter from the outside world.'

That's it, Toft whispered. Now anybody can attack him, he's not electric any more ... he's just shrinking and shrinking and doesn't know where to turn ... Toft curled up in the roach-net and started to describe it all for himself. He let the creature come to a valley where a toft lived who could make electric storms. The long valley was lit up by violet and white flashes, in the distance at first, then nearer and nearer . . .

*

Not a single fish had got caught in Grandpa-Grumble's contraption. He was dozing on the bridge with his hat over his nose. Beside him Mymble lay on the mat she had taken from in front of the stove and looked down into the running water. The Hemulen was sitting next to the letter-box painting big letters on a piece of plywood. He was writing 'Moominvalley' in mahogany stain.

'Who's that for?' Mymble asked. 'If anyone has walked as far as this he knows that he's here.'

'No, it's not for other people,' the Hemulen explained, 'it's for us.'

'Why?' asked Mymble.

'I don't know,' the Hemulen answered in surprise. He painted the last letter while he was thinking and then suggested: 'Perhaps just to make sure? There's something rather special about names, if you see what I mean.'

'No,' said Mymble.

The Hemulen took a large nail out of his pocket and began to nail the plywood to the parapet of the bridge. Grandpa-Grumble roused himself and muttered: 'Save the Ancestor . . .' And Snufkin came out of his tent and shouted: 'What are you doing? Stop at once!'

They had never seen Snufkin lose his self-control before, it scared and embarrassed them. Nobody looked at him. The Hemulen took the nail out.

'There's no need to feel hurt!' Snufkin called out petulantly. 'You know what I'm like!'

Even a hemulen should learn that a snufkin loathes notices, everything that reminds him of private property,

77

No entry, Off limits, Keep out – if one is the least bit interested in a snufkin one knows that notices are the only things that can make him angry, vulnerable and at the mercy of others. And now he felt ashamed! He had shouted and carried on and it was not to be forgiven, even if one took out all the nails in the world!

The Hemulen let the piece of plywood slide down into the river. The letters quickly darkened and became unreadable and the notice was carried away by the current down to the sea.

'Look,' the Hemulen said, 'there it goes. Perhaps it wasn't as important as I imagined.'

The Hemulen's voice had changed just a little. There was a little less respect in it, he had come closer to someone, and he had a right to. Snufkin didn't say anything, but stood quite still. Suddenly he ran up to the letter-box by the parapet, lifted the lid and looked inside, then ran on to the maple-tree and shoved his arm in a hole in the trunk.

Grandpa-Grumble stood up and shouted: 'Are you expecting a letter?'

Snufkin had reached the woodshed. He turned the chopping-block upside down. He went inside the woodshed and searched behind the little window-shelf above the carpenter's bench.

78

'Are you looking for your glasses?' asked Grandpa-Grumble with interest.

Snufkin walked on. He said: 'I want to look in peace.'

'Do you really!' exclaimed Grandpa-Grumble and followed as fast as he could. 'You're quite right. There was a time when I used to search for things and words and names the whole day long and the worst thing was when other people tried to help.' He grabbed Snufkin's coat and held on tight and said: 'Do you know what it was like all day? Like this: when did you see it last? Try and remember. When did it happen? Where did it happen? Ha ha, all that's over and done with. I'll forget what I like and lose just what I like. Now, I can tell you . . .'

'Grandpa-Grumble,' said Snufkin, 'the fish swim along the bank in the autumn. There aren't any fish in the middle of the river.'

'The brook,' corrected Grandpa-Grumble cheerfully. 'That was the first sensible thing I've heard today.' He went off immediately. Snufkin went on with his search. He was hunting for Moomintroll's good-bye letter, which had to be somewhere because a moomintroll never forgets to say good-bye. But all their hiding-places were empty.

Moomintroll was the only one who knew how to write to a snufkin. Brief and to the point. Nothing about promises and longings and sad things. And a joke to finish up with.

Snufkin went into the house and up to the second floor. He forced out the big knot in the banisters and that was empty, too.

'Empty!' said Fillyjonk behind him. 'If you're hunting for their valuables they're not in there. They're in the clothes-cupboard and it's locked.' She sat in the doorway of

her room with blankets round her legs and her feather-boa
right up round her nose.

'They never lock anything,' said Snufkin.

'It's cold!' Fillyjonk cried. 'Why don't you like me?
Why can't you find something for me to do?'

'You could go down into the kitchen,' Snufkin muttered,
'it's warmer there.'

Fillyjonk didn't answer. A very faint rumble of thunder
could be heard in the distance.

'They never lock anything,' Snufkin said again. He went
over to the clothes-cupboard and opened the door. The
cupboard was empty. He went downstairs without looking
behind him.

Fillyjonk got up slowly. She could see that the cupboard
was empty. But out of the dusty darkness came a ghastly,
strange smell – it was the suffocating sweet smell of decay.
Inside the cupboard there was nothing except a moth-eaten
kettle-holder made of wool, and a soft layer of grey dust.
Fillyjonk put her head inside, shivering as she did so.
Weren't those straggly little footmarks in the dust, quite
tiny ones, almost invisible . . .? Something had been living
in the cupboard and had been let out. The kind of thing that
crawls out when you turn a stone over, that crawls under
rotting plants, she knew, and now they were loose! They
had come out with scratching legs, with rattling backs and
fumbling feelers or crawling on soft white stomachs . . . She

screamed: 'Toft! Come here!' And Toft came out of the box-room, he was all crumpled up and confused and looked at her as though he didn't recognize her. He opened his nostrils, there was a very strong smell of electricity here, keen and pungent.

'They've got out!' Fillyjonk shouted. 'They have been living in there and now they've got out!'

The door of the clothes-cupboard swung open and Fillyjonk saw a movement, a glimpse of danger – she screamed! But it was only the mirror on the inside of the door. The cupboard was still empty. Toft came closer with his paws over his mouth, his eyes were round and jet black. The smell of electricity got stronger and stronger.

'I let it out,' he whispered. 'It does exist, and now I've let it out.'

'What have you let out?' Fillyjonk asked anxiously.

Toft shook his head. 'I don't know,' he said.

'But you must have seen them,' said Fillyjonk. 'Think carefully. What did they look like?'

But Toft ran back to the box-room and shut himself in. His heart was pounding furiously. So it was really true. The Creature had come. It was in the valley. He opened the book at the right place and spelt out the words as fast as he could: 'According to what we have reason to suppose, its constitution gradually adapted itself to these new surroundings and the necessity to master them little by little formed the conditions under which survival seemed possible. This existence, which we dare only characterize as a pure assumption, an hypothesis, continued its obscure development for an indeterminable period without its behaviour pattern in any way aligning itself with the course of events which we are accustomed to construe as normal . . .'

But I don't understand a thing, Toft whispered. It's all words, words . . . If they don't hurry up, everything will go wrong! He slumped over the book with his paws clutching his hair and went on describing things to himself, desperately and in a disordered fashion, for he knew that the Creature was getting smaller and smaller the whole time and couldn't really fend for itself.

The thunderstorm was getting closer and closer! The lightning was coming from all directions! The electric sparks flew all over the place and the Creature sensed it – now! And it grew and grew . . . and now there was more lightning, white and violet! The Creature became bigger and bigger. It became so big that it almost didn't need any family . . .

Then Toft felt better. He lay on his back and looked up at the skylight, which was full of grey clouds. He could hear the thunder rumbling in the distance. It sounded just like the growling noise you make in your throat just before you get really angry.

*

Step by step Fillyjonk went down the stairs. She supposed that the ghastly little things had not crawled off in different directions. It was more likely that they were all huddled together, a coherent mass waiting in some murky, damp corner. There they sat, quite silently, in one of the hidden and rotting holes of autumn. But perhaps not! Perhaps they were under the beds, in the desk drawers, in one's own shoes – they might be anywhere!

It isn't fair, Fillyjonk thought. Nothing like this happens to anyone in my circle of acquaintances, only to me! She ran down to the tent with long, anxious strides and fumbled desperately with the closed flaps, whispering

hoarsely: 'Open up open up for me ... it's me, Filly-jonk!'

She felt safer inside the tent, sank down on the sleeping-bag and put her arms round her knees. She said: 'They've got out. Someone let them out of the clothes-cupboard and they may be anywhere ... millions of horrid insects sitting and waiting ...'

'Has anybody else seen them?' Snufkin asked cautiously.

'Of course not,' Fillyjonk replied impatiently. 'It's *me* they're waiting for!'

Snufkin knocked out his pipe and tried to think of something to say. There was more thunder.

'Now don't start saying there's going to be a thunderstorm,' said Fillyjonk threateningly. 'And don't say that my insects have gone away or that they don't exist or that they're too small or too kind, for it won't help me one bit.'

Snufkin looked straight at her and said: 'There's one place where they'll never come. The kitchen. They never come into the kitchen.'

'Are you absolutely sure?' asked Fillyjonk sternly.

'I'm convinced of it,' answered Snufkin.

There was another peal of thunder, this time quite close. He looked at Fillyjonk and grinned. 'There's going to be a thunderstorm anyway,' he said.

There really was a big storm coming in from the sea. The lightning was white and violet, he had never seen so many or such beautiful flashes of lightning at one time. A sudden pall had descended on the valley. Fillyjonk lifted up her skirts and rushed back through the garden with leaps and bounds and shut the kitchen door behind her.

Snufkin sniffed the air, it felt as cold as steel. It smelt of electricity. The lightning was pouring down in great quivering streaks, parallel pillars of light, and the whole valley was lit up by their blinding flashes! Snufkin jumped up and

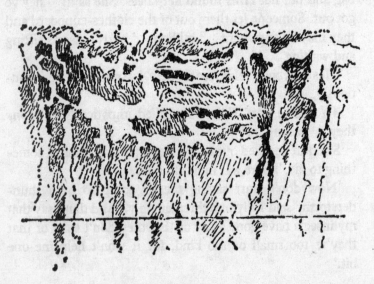

down with joy and admiration. He waited for the wind and the rain, but they didn't come. Only the thunder rumbled to and fro between the mountain peaks, enormous heavy spheres of sound, and there was a smell of burning everywhere. Then there was a last, triumphant earsplitting crash, and all was completely silent, without a single further flash.

That was a strange thunderstorm, Snufkin thought. I wonder where it struck.

At that moment he heard a terrible cry down by the bend in the river, and a cold shiver went up his spine. The lightning had struck Grandpa-Grumble!

When he got there, Grandpa-Grumble was jumping up and down. 'A fish! A fish!' he was shouting. 'I've caught a fish!' He was holding a perch between his paws and was beside himself with glee. 'Do you think it ought to be boiled or fried?' Grandpa-Grumble asked. 'Is there an oven to smoke it in? Is there anyone who can cook this fish without spoiling it?'

'Fillyjonk!' said Snufkin, and laughed. 'Fillyjonk's exactly the right person to do it!'

*

Fillyjonk stuck a quivering nose with all its whiskers standing on end round the door. She let Snufkin into the kitchen and closed the latch behind him. 'I think I've got over it,' she whispered.

Snufkin nodded his head. He knew she wasn't referring to the thunderstorm. 'Grandpa-Grumble has caught his first fish,' he said. 'And now the Hemulen says that only hemulens know how to cook fish. Is it true?'

'Of course it isn't true!' Fillyjonk exclaimed: 'Only fillyjonks know how to cook fish, and the Hemulen knows it!'

'But you'll never be able to make it enough for everybody,' Snufkin objected sadly.

'Indeed! You don't think I can,' said Fillyjonk, snatching the perch. 'I'd just like to see the fish I can't make do for six people!' She opened the kitchen door and said seriously: 'Now you must be off, I have to be alone when I'm cooking.'

'Aha!' shouted Grandpa-Grumble, who had been standing with his ear to the door. 'She likes cooking after all!'

Fillyjonk dropped the fish on the floor.

'But isn't it Fathers' Day?' Snufkin muttered.

'Are you sure?' Fillyjonk said disbelievingly. She looked sternly at Grandpa-Grumble and asked: 'Have you any children?'

'Certainly not,' answered Grandpa-Grumble. 'I don't like relatives! There are some great-great-grand-children somewhere, but I've forgotten them.'

Fillyjonk sighed. 'Why can't any of you behave normally,' she said. 'This house will drive me mad. Now off with both of you, I'm going to get dinner ready.'

She closed the latch of the door and picked up the perch. She looked round Moominmamma's kitchen and forgot everything except the right way to cook a fish.

*

During the short and violent thunderstorm Mymble had become completely and utterly electric. Sparks flew from her hair and every little bit of down on her arms and legs stood on end and quivered. Now I'm full of ferocity, she thought. I could do anything, but instead I'll do nothing. Isn't it marvellous to do just what one feels like? She curled

up on the eiderdown, feeling like a tiny flash of ball lightning, a ball of fire.

*

Toft was standing in the box-room looking through the skylight. He could see the flashes of lightning coming down into Moominvalley and he felt proud and carried away, and perhaps a little scared. It's my thunderstorm, Toft thought. I did it. At last I can describe things for myself so that they can actually be seen. I shall describe things for the last Nummulite, the little Radiolaria who belongs to the Protozoa family . . . I can make thunder roll and lightning flash, I am a toft whom nobody knows anything about.

He thought that he had punished Moominmamma with his thunderstorm and he decided to keep very quiet and not tell anything to anyone but himself and the Nummulite. Other people's electricity had nothing to do with him, he could feel it in the air but it was strange to him, he had his own storm all to himself. He wished that the whole valley had been empty with plenty of room for dreams, you need space and silence to be able to fashion things sufficiently carefully.

The bat on the ceiling was still asleep, it hadn't been at all bothered by the thunder.

The Hemulen called from the garden: 'Toft! Come and give me a hand!'

Toft left the box-room. He went down to the Hemulen, hidden by his silence, and by his hair, and nobody knew that he was holding electrical storms in his paws.

'Thunder, eh?' said the Hemulen. 'Were you scared?'

'No,' answered Toft.

CHAPTER 13

Music

THE Fillyjonk's fish was ready at exactly two o'clock. It was concealed in a huge, steaming light-brown pudding. The whole kitchen smelt convincingly and comfortingly of food. The kitchen had really become a kitchen, a safe room where one could take charge of things, the heart of the mysteries of the house and a source of confidence. No creepy-crawlies, no thunderstorms could reach it, for here Fillyjonk was in command. Fright and fainting-fits had retreated into the remotest corners of Fillyjonk's brain and the latch had been closed on them.

Thank goodness, she thought. I can't ever do any cleaning again, but at least I can cook. There's hope left after all! She opened the door and went out on to the veranda, she took down Moominmamma's shiny brass gong, held it in her paws and saw the reflection of her calm, triumphant face. She took the beater with its round wooden head covered with chamois-leather and struck the gong, 'Dong dong', and it resounded through the whole valley! 'Food! Come and get it!'

They all came rushing, shouting: 'What is it? What's happened?'

Fillyjonk answered calmly: 'Dinner is served.'

The kitchen table was set for six and Grandpa-Grumble's place was in the middle. Fillyjonk knew that he had been standing outside the window the whole time, anxious about his fish. Now he was allowed in.

'Food,' said Mymble. 'That's good. Gherkin and cinnamon biscuits don't really go together.'

'From now on,' said Fillyjonk, 'the pantry will be locked. The kitchen belongs to me. Now sit down and start before it gets cold.'

'Where's my fish?' asked Grandpa-Grumble.

'It's inside the food,' Fillyjonk answered.

'But I want to see it!' Grandpa-Grumble complained. 'It ought to have been whole and I would have eaten it all by myself!'

'Mercy me,' said Fillyjonk. 'I know it's Fathers' Day, but that's no reason for being selfish.' She thought that sometimes it's difficult to respect old age and comply with all the traditions that belong to a respectable way of living.

'I refuse to celebrate Fathers' Day,' Grandpa-Grumble insisted. 'Fathers' Day, and Mothers' Day and all the nice little Whompses' Day, I hate relatives! Can't we celebrate All Big Fishes' Day?'

'But this is real food,' said the Hemulen reproachfully. 'And we are sitting here as one big happy family. I've always said that Fillyjonk is the only one who can cook a fish.'

'Ha ha ha,' said Fillyjonk. She said 'ha ha ha' over again and looked at Snufkin.

They ate in silence. Fillyjonk went backwards and forwards between the stove and the table serving them, she poured out lemonade and was cross with anyone who dropped food down themselves and she was brimming over with well-being.

'Can't we have three cheers for Fathers' Day?' the Hemulen suddenly asked.

'We'll have no such thing,' said Grandpa-Grumble.

'I'm sorry,' said the Hemulen. 'I was only trying to be pleasant. Aren't we forgetting that Moominpappa is a father, too?' He looked gravely at them all and added: 'I have an idea. Why don't we, each one of us, prepare a surprise for Moominpappa before he comes home?'

Nobody said anything.

'Snufkin could mend the bathing-hut jetty,' the Hemulen went on. 'And Mymble could wash our clothes. And Fillyjonk could have a good spring-clean . . .'

Fillyjonk dropped a plate on the floor and cried: 'No. I shall never do any more cleaning!'

'Why not?' Mymble asked. 'You love cleaning.'

'I don't remember,' Fillyjonk muttered.

'You're quite right,' said Grandpa-Grumble. 'One should put all unpleasant things out of one's mind. Now I'm going to catch another fish and I shall eat it all myself.' He picked up his stick and went out, his napkin still hanging round his neck.

'Thank you for dinner,' said Toft, and bowed. And Snufkin said: 'That was a jolly good pudding.'

'Do you think so?' Fillyjonk answered with a faint smile, for her thoughts were elsewhere.

After dinner Snufkin lit his pipe and went down to the sea. He walked slowly and for the first time he felt lonely. He went right out to the bathing-hut and opened the squeaky narrow door. There was a smell of mould and seaweed and past summers, a melancholy smell. O houses,

houses, Snufkin thought. He sat on the steep little steps leading down into the water. The sea was calm and grey and there were no islands. Perhaps it isn't so difficult to find people who are hiding themselves and get them to come home again. The sea-chart shows all the islands. The dinghy could be made watertight. But why, thought Snufkin. Leave them alone. Perhaps they want to be left in peace, too.

Snufkin gave up looking for his five bars, they would have to be allowed to come when they wanted to. There were other songs anyway. Perhaps I'll play a little this evening, he thought.

*

It was late in the autumn and the evenings were very dark. Fillyjonk had never liked night-time. There's nothing

worse than looking into complete darkness, it is like walking straight out into eternity and not having anybody with you. That's why she put out the bucket of rubbish on the kitchen steps double quick and shut the door tight again, that's what she'd always done.

But tonight Fillyjonk stood on the steps and listened to the darkness. Snufkin was playing in his tent, a beautiful, vague tune. Fillyjonk wasn't musical, although neither she nor anybody else realized it. She listened breathlessly. She forgot all the awful things; tall and thin, she was silhouetted against the lighted kitchen, an easy prey to all the lurking dangers of the night. But nothing happened. When the melody was finished she gave a deep sigh, put down the bucket and went back into the house. It was Toft who emptied the bucket.

In the box-room Toft told himself: the Creature curled up by the big pool behind Moominpappa's tobacco bed and waited there. It was waiting until it would become so big and strong that it could never be disappointed, and until it cared about nothing but itself. End of chapter.

CHAPTER 14

Looking for the Family

IT was taken for granted that no one slept in Moomin-mamma's room or in Moominpappa's room. Because she was fond of the morning, Moominmamma's room faced east and Moominpappa's faced west because the evening sky used to make him feel wistful.

One day at dusk the Hemulen crept up to Moomin-pappa's room and stood respectfully in the doorway. It was quite a small room with a sloping ceiling, a place where one could be by oneself. Or a place where one could be got out of the way. On the blue walls Moominpappa had hung up curiously-shaped branches and he had stuck trouser-buttons on some of them. There was a calendar with a picture of a shipwreck and a piece of board saying Haig's Whisky hung over the bed. On the desk there were some peculiar stones, a nugget of gold and a mass of the sort of odds and ends one leaves behind at the last minute when one goes on a journey. Under the mirror there was a model of a lighthouse with a pointed roof, a little inlaid wooden door and a railing of brass nails round the lamp-room. There was even a ladder which Moominpappa had

94

made out of copper wire. He had pasted silver paper on all the windows.

The Hemulen looked at all this and tried to remember what Moominpappa was like. He tried to remember the things they had done together and what they had talked about, but he couldn't. Then he went over to the window and looked out at the garden. The shells round the dead flower-beds shone in the twilight and in the west the sky was yellow. The big maple-tree was coal-black against the sunset – the Hemulen was looking at exactly what Moominpappa looked at in the autumn twilight.

Then all of a sudden the Hemulen knew what he would do, he would build a house for Moominpappa in the big maple-tree! He was so pleased with this idea that he started to laugh! A tree-house, of course! High above the ground between the strong black branches far away from the family, free and full of adventure and with a storm lantern on the roof; there they would sit and listen to the south-wester making the walls creak and talk to each other at last. The Hemulen rushed out into the hall and called: 'Toft!'

Toft came out of his box-room.

'Have you been reading again?' the Hemulen asked. 'It's dangerous to read too much. Listen, do you like pulling out nails, eh?'

'I don't think so,' answered Toft.

'If anything is going to get done,' the Hemulen explained, 'one person does the building and the other carries the planks. Or one knocks in new nails and the other one pulls out old nails. Do you understand?'

Toft just looked. He knew that he was the other one.

They went down to the woodshed and Toft began to pull out nails. They were old boards and planks which the

Family had collected on the beach, the grey timber was hard and compact and the nails rusted in. The Hemulen went on to the maple-tree, and looked up thoughtfully.

Toft prised the nails loose and pulled. The sunset was a fiery yellow just before the sun went down. He told himself about the Creature, and he could do it better and better, not in words any longer but in pictures. Words are dangerous things and the Creature had reached a vital point in its development, it was just about to change. It didn't hide itself any longer, it watched and listened, it slid like a dark shadow towards the edge of the forest, very intently and not at all afraid . . .

'Do you like pulling out nails?' Mymble asked behind him. She was sitting on the chopping-block.

'What?' said Toft.

'You don't like pulling out nails, but you do it all the same,' said Mymble. 'I wonder why?'

Toft looked at her and kept quiet. Mymble smelt of peppermints.

'And you don't like the Hemulen either,' she went on.

'I've never given it a thought,' Toft muttered deprecatingly, and immediately started to think whether he liked the Hemulen or not.

Mymble jumped down from the chopping-block and went away. The twilight suddenly deepened and a grey mist rose over the river, it was very cold.

'Open up,' shouted Mymble outside the kitchen door. 'I want to warm myself in your kitchen.'

It was the first time anybody had said 'your kitchen' and Fillyjonk opened the door at once. 'You can sit on my bed, but mind you don't crumple the bedspread.'

Mymble curled up on the bed which had been pushed between the stove and the sink and Fillyjonk went on

making the bread pudding for the next day. She had found a bag of old crusts that the family had been saving for the birds. It was warm in the kitchen, the fire crackled in the stove, throwing flickering shadows on the ceiling.

'Right now it's just like it always used to be,' said Mymble to herself.

'You mean like it was in Moominmamma's day,' said Fillyjonk to be precise but without thinking.

'No, not at all,' Mymble answered. 'Just the stove.'

Fillyjonk went on with the bread pudding, going backwards and forwards in the kitchen on her high heels, and her thoughts suddenly became anxious and uncertain. 'What do you mean?' she asked.

'Moominmamma used to whistle while she was cooking,' Mymble said. 'Everything was a little just anyhow ... I don't know – it was different. Sometimes they took their food with them and went somewhere, and sometimes they didn't eat at all . . .' She put her arm over her head in order to go to sleep.

'I should imagine that I know Moominmamma considerably better than you do,' Fillyjonk said. She greased the baking-tin, threw in the last of the soup from the day before and surreptitiously added a few boiled potatoes which were no longer what they had once been; she got more and more agitated and in the end she dashed over to the sleeping Mymble and shouted: 'You wouldn't lie there sleeping if you knew what I know!'

Mymble woke up and lay still, looking at Fillyjonk.

'You've no idea,' whispered Fillyjonk intensely. 'You've no idea what has broken loose in this valley! Horrid things have been let out of the clothes-cupboard upstairs and they're everywhere!' Mymble sat up and asked: 'Is that why you've got fly-paper round your boots?' She yawned and rubbed her nose. She turned round in the doorway and said: 'Don't fuss, there's nothing here that's worse than we are ourselves.'

'Is she angry?' Grandpa-Grumble asked from the drawing-room.

'She's scared,' answered Mymble and went up the stairs. 'She's scared of something in the clothes-cupboard.'

It was now quite dark outside. They had all got used to going to bed when it got dark, and they slept for a long time, longer and longer as the days drew in. Toft crept in like a shadow and gave a mumbled good night and Hemulen turned his nose to the wall. He had decided to build a cupola on the top of Moominpappa's tree-house. He could paint it green and perhaps put gold stars on it. There was generally some gold paint in Moominmamma's desk and he had seen a tin of bronze paint in the woodshed.

When they were all asleep, Grandpa-Grumble climbed

the stairs with a candle. He stopped outside the big
clothes-cupboard and whispered: 'Are you there? I know
you're there.' He opened the cupboard very gently, and the
door with the mirror swung open.

The candle flame was very small and gave very little
light in the hall, but Grandpa-Grumble could see the Ancestor quite clearly in front of him. He was wearing a hat
and carried a stick and looked highly improbable. His
dressing-gown was too long and he was wearing gaiters.

But no glasses. Grandpa-Grumble took a step forward and the Ancestor did the same thing.

'So you don't live in the stove any longer,' said Grandpa-Grumble. 'How old are you? Don't you ever wear glasses?' He was very excited and thumped with his stick on the floor to give emphasis to what he was saying. The Ancestor did the same, but didn't answer.

He's deaf, said Grandpa-Grumble to himself. A stone-deaf old bag of bones. But in any case it's nice to meet someone who knows what it feels like to be old. He remained there staring at the Ancestor for a long time. The Ancestor did the same. They parted with feelings of mutual esteem.

CHAPTER 15

Nummulite

THE days were growing shorter and colder. It didn't rain very often. The sun shone down into the valley for a short while each day and the bare trees threw shadows on the ground but in the morning and in the evening everything lay in half-light and then night came. They never saw the sun go down but they did see the yellow glow of the sunset in the sky and the sharp outlines of the mountains all round – it was like living in a well.

The Hemulen and Toft were building Moominpappa's tree-house. Grandpa-Grumble caught a couple of fish every day and Fillyjonk had begun to whistle.

It was an autumn without storms and the big thunderstorm didn't come back, but rolled past in the distance with a faint rumbling sound that made the silence in the valley seem even deeper. Only Toft knew that every time the thunder was heard the Creature grew and lost a bit more of its shyness. It was fairly big now and had changed a lot, it had opened its mouth and had shown its teeth. One evening in the yellow light of sunset the Creature leant over the water and saw its own white teeth for the first time. It opened its mouth and yawned, then snapped its mouth shut and gnashed its teeth a bit, and thought: I don't need anyone now, I've got teeth.

In the end Toft didn't dare make the Creature any bigger. He made all the pictures vanish, but the thunder continued to rumble over the sea and Toft could feel that the Creature was now growing on its own.

Toft found it difficult to go to sleep at night without first telling something to himself because he'd been doing it for so long. He read and read in his book and understood less and less. Now they were talking about what the Creature looked like inside, and it was boring.

One evening Fillyjonk tapped on the box-room door, opened it cautiously and said: 'Hallo there!'

Toft looked up from his book and waited.

The big Fillyjonk sat down on the floor beside him, put her head on one side and said: 'What are you reading?'

'A book,' Toft answered.

Fillyjonk took a deep breath and took the plunge: 'It isn't always easy to be small and not have a mummy, is it?'

Toft hid himself in his chair. He felt ashamed of her and didn't answer.

Fillyjonk reached out her paw and then drew it back. She said very sincerely: 'Yesterday evening I suddenly thought of you. What is your name again?'

'Toft,' said Toft.

'Toft,' Fillyjonk repeated. 'A lovely name.' She desperately searched for words and wished she knew a little more about children and liked them. In the end she said: 'Are you warm enough? Are you all right here?'

'Yes, thank you,' said Toft.

Fillyjonk tried to look straight into his eyes and asked imploringly: 'Are you really sure?'

Toft drew back a bit, she smelt of fear. Hastily he said: 'A blanket, perhaps.'

Fillyjonk got up immediately. 'And you shall have one,' she exclaimed. 'Just wait, it won't take a minute . . .' He heard her running down the stairs and coming back again. She had a blanket with her.

'Thank you very much,' Toft said, and bowed. 'It's a very good blanket.'

Fillyjonk smiled. 'Oh, don't mention it!' she said. 'Moominmamma would have done the same.' She dropped the blanket on the floor, hesitated a little, and then went away.

Toft folded the blanket up as neatly as he could and put it at the back of the shelf, he crept into the roach-net and tried to go on reading. It was no good. He understood less and less, and read the same sentence many times over without knowing what he was reading. In the end he put the book down, blew out his candle and went out.

It was difficult to find the crystal ball. He walked the wrong way, floundering around among the tree-trunks as if the garden was a strange place to him. At last the crystal ball appeared out of the darkness, but its blue light had gone out and it was full of fog, thick dark fog which was hardly any lighter than the night itself. Inside the magic ball the fog quickly floated past, disappeared, was sucked in, and went round and round, more and more fog in deep, darkening spirals.

Toft walked along the river and passed Moominpappa's tobacco bed. He stepped in under the spruce-trees by the big pool, the withered reeds rustled on all sides and his shoes sank into the boggy ground.

'Are you there?' he called softly. 'Little Nummulite, how are you?'

Then the Creature growled at him from the darkness.

Horror-stricken, Toft rushed blindly away, stumbling and falling and dragging himself up again until he reached the tent. It shone like a calm green light in the night. Inside Snufkin was playing softly to himself.

'It's me,' Toft whispered. He went inside the tent, where he'd never been before. It smelt nice inside – of pipe-tobacco and earth. Beside the sleeping-bag was a candle on a sugar box and the floor was covered with wood-shavings.

'It's going to be a wooden-spoon,' Snufkin said. 'Were you frightened by something?'

'There is no family any longer,' answered Toft. 'They've deceived me.'

'I don't believe that,' said Snufkin. 'Perhaps they just want to be in peace for a while.' He picked up his thermos flask and filled two mugs with tea. 'There's the sugar,' he said. 'They're sure to come home some time.'

'Some time!' exclaimed Toft. 'She must come now, she's the only one I care about!'

Snufkin shrugged his shoulders. He made two sandwiches and said: 'I wonder what it is that Moominmamma cares about . . .'

Toft said no more. As he was leaving Snufkin called after him: 'You want to be careful not to let things get too big.'

Then the sound of the mouth-organ could be heard again. Fillyjonk stood on the kitchen steps with her bucket of rubbish at her side, listening. Toft made a detour round her and slunk stealthily into the house.

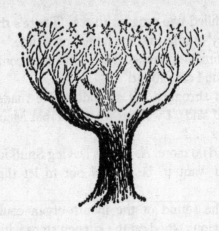

CHAPTER 16

Picnic

SNUFKIN was summoned to Sunday dinner on the following day. It was two o'clock, quarter past two and Fillyjonk still hadn't called them to table. When half past two came Snufkin put a new feather in his hat and went to see what was up. The kitchen table was standing by the steps and the Hemulen and Toft were carrying chairs out.

'It's a picnic,' Grandpa-Grumble explained gloomily. 'She says that today's the day when we must do just what we feel like doing.'

Fillyjonk came out with the food. It was oatmeal porridge. A gentle but cold wind swept through the valley and made a skin on the porridge.

'Now help yourself and don't be shy,' said Fillyjonk to Toft and patted him on the head.

'What do we have to eat outside for?' Grandpa-Grumble complained. He pushed the skin to the side of his plate.

'You must eat the skin, too,' Fillyjonk remarked.

'Why can't we eat in the kitchen?' said Grandpa-Grumble.

'Sometimes one does just what occurs to one. One takes one's food with one or perhaps one doesn't eat anything at all. It's fun!'

The table was crooked on the uneven ground. The Hemulen held his plate in his paws. 'There's something that's bothering me,' he said. 'The cupola isn't going well. Toft saws the wood according to my instructions but it's never right. And when you saw a little more off the plank, it's too short and falls off. Do you see what I mean?'

'What about making an ordinary roof?' suggested Snufkin.

'That would fall off, too,' said Hemulen.

'I hate skin on oatmeal porridge,' said Grandpa-Grumble.

'Of course, there's another possibility,' the Hemulen went on. 'Not to have a roof at all! I have been sitting here thinking that perhaps Moominpappa would prefer to look at the stars. Don't you think he would rather look at the stars?'

Toft suddenly exclaimed: 'That's what *you* think! What do *you* know about what Moominpappa likes?'

They all stopped eating and stared at him.

Toft clutched the tablecloth and shouted: 'You please yourself what you do in any case! Why do you have to make such *big* things?'

'Well, what do you know!' said Mymble in astonishment. 'Toft's baring his teeth!'

Toft got up so violently that his chair fell over. He hid himself under the table.

'Really! Toft, who is generally so well-behaved,' Fillyjonk said stiffly. 'And on a picnic, too!'

'Listen, Fillyjonk,' said Mymble seriously. 'I don't think moving the kitchen table outdoors makes one a moominmamma.'

Fillyjonk stood up and cried: 'Moominmamma! Moominmamma! That's all I hear! What's so special about her? A slovenly family, the whole lot of them! They don't even clean their own house, even though they *can* clean, and they don't even leave the briefest note behind although they knew that we ... although they knew that ...' She stopped, helpless.

'A note!' declared Grandpa-Grumble. 'I found a note somewhere and I hid it somewhere.'

'What? Where did you hide it?' Snufkin demanded.

Now they all stood up.

'Somewhere,' Grandpa-Grumble muttered. 'I think I'll go fishing. I'm not enjoying this picnic. It's no fun.'

'Now think carefully,' the Hemulen begged. 'Try and remember. We'll help you. When did you see it last, what? Where would you hide it now if you'd only just found it?'

'I am on holiday,' Grandpa-Grumble said sulkily. 'I can forget what I like. It's marvellous to forget. I intend to forget everything except one or two nice things that are important. I shall go and have a chat with my friend the Ancestor. He knows. *You* only think, *we* know.'

The Ancestor looked just the same as usual, except that he had a napkin round his neck.

'Hallo,' said Grandpa-Grumble, 'I'm really angry. Do you know what they've done to me?' He waited a while. The Ancestor shook his head slowly and stamped his feet.

'You're right,' said Grandpa-Grumble. 'They have ruined my holiday. Here I am, feeling proud that I've managed to forget as much as I have and suddenly I'm supposed to start *remembering* things! It gives me a pain in the stomach. I'm so angry that I almost do *have* a pain in the stomach.'

For the first time Grandpa-Grumble remembered his medicines. But he couldn't remember where he had put them.

*

'They were in a basket,' the Hemulen repeated. 'He said that he had them in a basket. And it isn't in the drawing-room.'

'Perhaps he's left it somewhere in the garden,' said Mymble.

Fillyjonk exclaimed: 'He says it's our fault! How can it be my fault? The only thing I've done is make him hot blackcurrant juice. He liked it!' She gave Mymble a wry look and added: 'I know that Moominmamma usually makes hot blackcurrant juice whenever anybody's ill, but I did it all the same.'

'Now, keep calm everybody,' said the Hemulen. 'I'll tell you what you must do. It's a question of medicine bottles and brandy, a note and eight pairs of glasses. We'll divide the valley and the house into different parts and then everyone . . .'

'Yes, yes, yes,' said Fillyjonk. She put her nose round the drawing-room door and asked anxiously: 'How do you feel now?'

'Bad,' said Grandpa-Grumble. 'This is what happens when there's skin on the oatmeal porridge and I'm not left

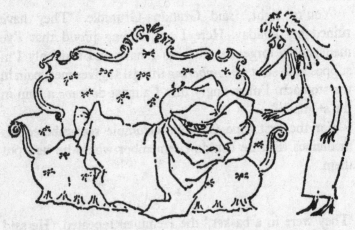

in peace to forget things.' He was lying on the drawing-room sofa under a pile of blankets and had his hat on.

'How old are you, actually?' Fillyjonk asked cautiously.

'I have no intention of dying,' Grandpa-Grumble declared cheerfully. 'How old are you yourself?'

Fillyjonk disappeared. Doors were opened and shut all over the house, the garden was full of the sound of shouts and running footsteps. Nobody thought of anything but Grandpa-Grumble. That basket might be anywhere, he thought not without a certain satisfaction. His stomach had settled.

Mymble came in and sat on the edge of his sick-bed. 'Listen, Grandpa-Grumble,' she said. 'You're just as well as I am and you know it.'

'Possibly,' Grandpa-Grumble answered. 'But I shan't get up until I know that I can have a party! Quite a small party for old people who have recovered.'

'Or a big party for mymbles who want to dance,' said Mymble thoughtfully.

'Not at all!' Grandpa-Grumble exclaimed. 'A huge party for me and the Ancestor. He hasn't had a party for a hundred years, and now he's sitting in the clothes-cupboard feeling sorry for himself.'

'If you believe that you'd believe anything,' said Mymble with a grin.

'It's found!' the Hemulen shouted outside. The door flew open and the drawing-room was suddenly full of people and movement. 'The basket was under the veranda!' the Hemulen exclaimed. 'And the brandy was on the other side of the river!'

'Brook,' corrected Grandpa-Grumble. 'I'll have the brandy first.' Fillyjonk poured out a little drop and they all watched him carefully while he drank it down.

'Do you want a little of each medicine or only one kind?' Fillyjonk asked.

'None at all,' Grandpa-Grumble answered, and fell back among the cushions with a sigh. 'Don't ever again mention things I don't like to hear. And I shan't get really well before I've been given a party . . .'

'Take off his boots,' said the Hemulen. 'Toft, take off his boots. It's the first thing to do when anybody's got a stomach-ache.'

Toft unlaced Grandpa-Grumble's boots and took them off. He took a crumpled up piece of white paper out of one of them.

'The note!' Snufkin exclaimed. He smoothed out the paper carefully and read:

'Please do not light a fire in the stove because that's where the Ancestor lives. – Moominmamma.'

CHAPTER 17

Preparations

FILLYJONK said nothing more about what had been living in the clothes-cupboard, but tried to fill her head with small, fussy thoughts of the kind she was used to. But at night she could hear the faint, hardly distinguishable sounds that occur when something is crawling inside the wallpaper, sometimes a scurrying sound along the wainscot, and once a death-watch beetle had been ticking over the head of her bed.

The best things in the whole day were being able to bang the gong and put the rubbish bucket on the steps after dark. Snufkin played almost every evening and Fillyjonk had learnt his tunes. But she only whistled when she was sure that no one would hear her.

One evening she was sitting by the stove trying to find some excuse for not going to bed.

'Are you asleep?' asked Mymble outside the door. She came in without waiting for an answer and said: 'I need some rainwater to wash my hair.'

'Really,' said Fillyjonk. 'I should have thought that river

water would have done just as well. It's in the middle bucket. That one's spring water. But you can rinse your hair with rainwater if you insist. Don't spill any on the floor.'

'You seem to be yourself again,' Mymble declared and put the water on the stove. 'Actually, you're nicer that way. I shall wear my hair down for the party.'

'What party?' said Fillyjonk sharply.

'The party for Grandpa-Grumble,' Mymble answered. 'Didn't you know that we're having a party in the kitchen tomorrow?'

'You don't mean to say so! It's news to me!' Fillyjonk exclaimed. 'That's certainly something worth knowing! It's just exactly what one should do when one is shut in together, washed ashore, wind-blown, rain-drenched – one has a party and in the middle of the party the lights go out and when they go on again there is One Less in the House.'

Mymble looked at Fillyjonk with new interest. 'Sometimes you're very surprising,' she said. 'That wasn't bad at all. And then one after another vanishes and in the end only the cat is left, washing itself on their graves!'

Fillyjonk shuddered. 'I think your water is hot,' she said. 'There's no cat here.'

'It would be easy to get one,' said Mymble with a grin. 'You just imagine it and there you are, you've got a cat!' She took the saucepan off the stove and opened the door with her elbow. 'Good night,' she said. 'And don't forget to put your hair in curlers. And the Hemulen said that you were the one to decorate the kitchen because you're the most artistic.' Then Mymble went away and closed the door behind her quite niftily with her foot.

Fillyjonk's heart started pounding. She was artistic, the Hemulen had said that she was artistic. What a wonder-

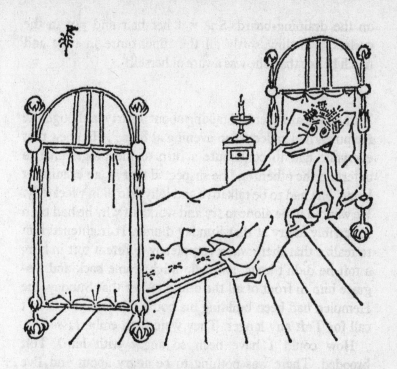

ful word! She whispered it over and over again to herself.

In the silence of the night Fillyjonk took her kitchen lamp and went to hunt for the decorations in the cupboard above Moominmamma's wardrobe. The cardboard box with the Japanese lanterns and the ribbon was in its usual place on top on the right, they were all jumbled up and covered in candlewax. The Easter ornaments, old birthday wrapping-papers with rose patterns, still had greetings on them: 'To my darling Pappa,' 'Happy Birthday dear Hemulen,' 'With love and kisses this we send, To Little My our own dear Friend.' 'To Gaffsie, with best wishes.' They hadn't liked Gaffsie as much.

Then she came across the paper streamers. Fillyjonk carried everything down to the kitchen and spread it all out on the draining-board. She wet her hair and put in the curlers, whistling softly all the time, quite in tune and much better than she was aware of herself.

*

Toft had heard them all talking about a party, although the Hemulen had called it 'an evening at home'. He knew that everyone had to contribute a turn to the programme to entertain the others and he suspected that at 'an evening at home' one had to be talkative and jolly. He didn't feel jolly. He wanted to be alone to try and work out why he had been so terribly angry at that Sunday dinner. It frightened him to realize that there was a completely different toft in him, a toft he didn't know and who might come back and disgrace him in front of all the others. After that Sunday, the Hemulen had been building his house all alone. He didn't call for Toft any longer. They were both embarrassed.

How could I have been so angry with him? Toft brooded. There was nothing to be angry about and I've never been angry before. It just came over me, like something rising and overflowing, like a waterfall! And I'm so good-natured, too.

The good-natured Toft went down to the river for water. He filled the bucket and put it down outside the tent. Snufkin was sitting inside making a wooden-spoon, or perhaps nothing at all, just keeping quiet and knowing about things better than anyone else. Everything Snufkin said sounded so good, so right, and when you were alone again you didn't understand what he meant and felt too shy to go back and ask. Or sometimes he didn't answer your questions at all but talked about tea or the weather and chewed his pipe and made that awful vague noise, making you feel you'd asked something quite dreadful.

I wonder why they all admire him, Toft thought seriously. Of course, it's stylish to smoke a pipe. Perhaps they admire him because he walks away and shuts himself up. But I do the same and nobody thinks anything of it. What's wrong is that I'm too small. Toft strolled farther down the garden, right down to the big pool, and thought: I don't want friends who are kind without really liking me and I don't want anybody who is kind just so as not to be unpleasant. And I don't want anybody who is scared. I want somebody who is never scared and who really likes me. I want a mamma!

The big pool was a gloomy place in the autumn, a place to hide oneself and wait. But Toft had a feeling that the Creature wasn't there any longer. It had gone. It had gnashed its new teeth and made off. And it was he, Toft, who had given the Creature its teeth.

Grandpa-Grumble sat dozing on the bridge. As Toft passed him, he roused himself and shouted: 'We're having a party! A big party in my honour!'

Toft tried to slip past him, but Grandpa-Grumble caught hold of him with his stick. 'You must listen to me,' he said. 'I've told the Hemulen that the Ancestor is my best friend and hadn't had a party for a hundred years, and he must be invited! As guest of honour! "Yes, yes, yes," the Hemulen says. But I'm telling all of you that I shan't come to the party without the Ancestor! Do you understand?'

'Yes,' muttered Toft. 'I understand.' But he was thinking about the Creature.

Mymble was sitting on the veranda combing her hair in the pale sunshine. 'Hallo, Toft,' she said. 'Have you got your turn ready?'

'I can't do anything,' answered Toft, turning away.

'Come here,' said Mymble. 'Your hair needs combing.'

Toft placed himself in front of her obediently and Mymble started to comb his scruffy hair. 'If only you combed it for ten minutes every day it wouldn't be so bad,' she said. 'It falls well, and it's a nice colour. So you can't do anything? Well, you were angry, weren't you? But then you crept under the table and spoilt it all.'

Toft stood still, he liked having his hair combed. 'Mymble,' he said shyly. 'Where would you go if you were a great big angry animal?'

Mymble answered immediately: 'To the bottom of the back garden in those horrid trees behind the kitchen. That's where they went to when they were angry.' She went on combing, and Toft said: 'You mean when you are angry.'

'No. The family,' Mymble said. 'They went to the back

garden when they were fed up and angry and wanted a bit of peace and quiet.'

Toft took a step backwards and cried: 'It's not true! They were never angry!'

'Stand still,' said Mymble. 'How do you think I can comb your hair if you jump about like that? And I can tell you that both Moominpappa and Moominmamma got terribly tired of one another from time to time. Come here.'

'I won't!' exclaimed Toft. 'Moominmamma was never like that! She was the same all the time!' He pulled open the drawing-room door and slammed it behind him. Mymble was lying. She didn't know anything about Moominmamma. She didn't know that it was impossible for a mamma to behave badly.

*

Fillyjonk hung up the last streamer, a blue one. She stepped backwards and looked at her kitchen. It was the

dirtiest and dustiest in the whole world, but oh! how artist-
ically it was decorated! They were to have an early dinner on
the veranda, a heated-up fish soup, and after seven o'clock
there were to be Welsh rarebits and cider. She had found
the cider in Moominpappa's wardrobe and the tin with the
cheese rinds on the top shelf in the pantry. It was labelled
'for field mice'.

Fillyjonk put the napkins on the table with great ele-
gance, each napkin was shaped like a swan (not for Snufkin
of course, he always refused to use a napkin). She whistled
softly, her forehead was covered with a mass of tight little
curls and it was easy to see that she had put make-up on
her eyebrows. Nothing was crawling behind the wallpaper,
nothing was scuttling along the wainscot, the death-watch
beetle had stopped ticking. She had no time for them just
now, she had to think of her number on the programme. A
shadow-play: 'The Returning Family'. It'll be very dra-
matic, Fillyjonk thought calmly. They'll love it. She
latched the kitchen door and the drawing-room door. She
laid out some cartridge-paper on the draining-board and
started to draw. The picture was to show four people in a
boat. Two big people, one smaller and one quite tiny. The
tiny one sat in the prow of the boat. The drawing didn't
turn out quite as Fillyjonk had imagined it and she hadn't
got a rubber. But the idea was the important thing. When
the picture was ready she cut it out and nailed the boat to
the broom handle. She worked quickly and deliberately,
whistling all the time, not Snufkin's songs but her own.
Actually, Fillyjonk whistled much better than she could
draw or knock in nails.

Then she lit the kitchen lamp, it was dusk. But today it
wasn't a melancholy twilight, it was full of promise. The
lamp threw a faint light on the wall, she lifted up the broom

with the silhouette of the family in the boat and the shadow appeared on the wallpaper. Now she must get a sheet, the white surface on which they were going to sail out across the sea . . .

'Open the door!' shouted Grandpa-Grumble outside the drawing-room. Fillyjonk opened it a crack and said: 'Too early!'

'Things are happening here!' Grandpa-Grumble whispered. 'He's been invited and got an invitation card! In the clothes-cupboard. And you must put this in the place of honour.' He shoved in a big wet bouquet tied up with leaves and moss. Fillyjonk looked at the withered plants and wrinkled her nose. 'No bacteria in my kitchen,' she said.

'But it's maple! They've all been washed in the brook,' objected Grandpa-Grumble.

'Bacteria love water,' Fillyjonk pointed out. 'Have you taken your medicines?'

'Do you think that one needs to take medicine at a party?' said Grandpa-Grumble scornfully. 'I have forgotten them. And do you know what has happened? I've lost all my glasses again!'

'Congratulations,' said Fillyjonk dryly. 'I suggest you send this bouquet straight to the clothes-cupboard. It would be politer.' She shut the door with a bang.

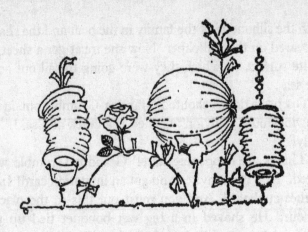

CHAPTER 18

Absent Friends

THE lanterns were all lit, red ones, yellow ones and green ones, all admiring their soft reflections in the dark window-panes. The guests came into the kitchen, greeted each other solemnly and sat down. But the Hemulen remained standing behind his chair. He said: 'This is "an evening at home" held in the spirit of the family. I beg to be allowed to commence this evening with a poem I have written particularly for this unique occasion and which I have dedicated to Moominpappa.' He took out a piece of paper and began to declaim, he was very moved:

'Oh say, where lies true lasting happiness?
In evening rest? In friendly glance? 'Tis more:
In sailing from the mire, the reeds, the mass,
The mighty ocean's vastness to adore.
Oh what is life? 'tis nothing but a dream,
A vast and enigmatic flowing stream.
Such tender feelings fill my heaving breast

I know not how or where they'll come to rest;
My cares are multitudinous and sore,
I long to feel the friendly rudder in my paw.'

They all clapped.
'Multitudinous,' Grandpa-Grumble repeated. 'That's
nice. Just the way people used to talk when I was young.'
'Wait!' the Hemulen said. 'It's not me you should ap-
plaud. Let us observe half-a-minute's silence to show our
appreciation of the Moomin family. We are eating their
food – or rather, what is left of it – we walk beneath their
trees, it is in the spirit of tolerance, companionship and *joie
de vivre* created by them that we are living. A minute's
silence!'
'You said half-a-minute,' Grandpa-Grumble muttered
and began to count the seconds. They all stood up and
raised their glasses, it was a solemn moment. 'Twenty-
four, twenty-five, twenty-six ...' Grandpa-Grumble
counted, his legs felt a little tired today. They ought to
have been his seconds, it was his party and not the family's
after all. They hadn't had a stomach-ache. And he was
annoyed with the Ancestor for not coming on time.
While the guests were honouring the Moomin family in
silence, a faint thumping sound could be heard outside
somewhere near the kitchen steps. It sounded as though
something was groping its way up the wall. Fillyjonk shot a
glance at the door – it was latched. She caught Toft's eye.
They both lifted their noses and sniffed, but said
nothing.
'Cheers!' the Hemulen exclaimed. 'Here's to good companionship!' They all drank. The glasses were the smallest
and the best ones, the ones with decorated rims. Then they
sat down.

'And now,' said the Hemulen, 'the programme will continue with the least significant of us. It's only fair that the last shall be first, eh, Toft?'

Toft opened his book somewhere towards the end. He read, rather quietly, pausing every time before a long word: 'Page two hundred and twenty-seven. It is exceptional that a form of life of this species we have attempted to reconstruct has retained its graminivorous nature in a purely physiological sense simultaneously with a continuing aggressivity of attitude towards its environment. No changes occurred with regard to the sharpening of its reflexes, its speed, its strength, or any of the other aspects of the predatory instincts normally associated with the development of carnivores. The teeth show blunt mastication surfaces, the claws are completely rudimentary and vision negligible. On the other hand, the total volume of the individual of this species has increased to an astonishing extent, which must, quite simply, have subjected it to certain inconveniences, bearing in mind the fact that it had for millennia dreamed away its life in concealed cracks and crevices. In this case we are faced with the astonishing phenomenon of a form of development which unites all the identifiable characteristics of the indolent graminivorous species with an ineffective and completely inexplicable aggressivity.'

'What was that last word?' Grandpa-Grumble asked, having been sitting with his paw to his ear the whole time. There was nothing wrong with his hearing as long as he knew what people were going to say. One almost knows what people are going to say.

'Aggressivity,' Mymble answered rather loudly.

'Don't shout at me, I'm not deaf,' Grandpa-Grumble said automatically. 'And what's that?'

'It's what one shows when one is angry,' explained Fillyjonk.

'Aha,' said Grandpa-Grumble, 'then I understand the whole thing. Has anyone else written anything or are we going to start the programme soon?' He started to feel uneasy about the Ancestor. Perhaps he, too, was tired and stiff, perhaps he hadn't managed the stairs. Perhaps he felt insulted, or perhaps he had fallen asleep. Anyway, something must be wrong, Grandpa-Grumble thought, somewhat vexed. They're always impossible when they pass a hundred. Rude, too . . .

'Mymble!' the Hemulen announced loudly. 'Allow me to present Mymble!'

Mymble walked to the middle of the floor, looking very shy and self-conscious. Her hair reached to her knees, and it was obvious that the hair-washing had been a success. She nodded briefly to Snufkin and he started to play. He played very softly. Mymble raised her arms and circled with short, hesitant steps. Shoo, shoo, tiddledidoo, said the mouth-organ; imperceptibly the music moved into a tune, became more and more lively and Mymble quickened her steps, the kitchen was full of music and movement and her long red hair looked like flying sunshine. It was all so

beautiful and jolly! No one heard the Creature, huge and heavy, creeping round and round the house without knowing what it wanted. The guests beat time with their feet and sang tiddledidi, tiddledidoo, Mymble kicked off her boots, threw her scarf on the floor, the paper streamers fluttered in the warmth from the stove, everybody clapped their paws and Snufkin stopped playing with a loud cry! Mymble laughed with self-satisfied pride.

Everybody shouted: 'Bravo! bravo!' and the Hemulen said with genuine admiration: 'Thank you ever so much.'

'Don't thank me,' Mymble answered. 'I can't stop myself. You ought to do the same thing!'

Fillyjonk stood up and said: 'Not being able to stop doing something and having to do it don't go together. I don't think that what one should do is the same thing as not being able to stop oneself doing it . . .' They all reached for their glasses, thinking that Fillyjonk was going to make a speech. When nothing came of it they all started to shout for more music. But Grandpa-Grumble was no longer interested, he sat fiddling with his napkin, rolling it up until it became thicker and smaller. The most likely thing was that the Ancestor felt hurt. A guest of honour ought to be escorted to a party, as people used to do in the old days. They had all behaved very badly.

Suddenly Grandpa-Grumble stood up and banged on the table. 'We have behaved very badly,' he said. 'We've started the party without our guest of honour and we haven't escorted him down the stairs. You're all too young and know nothing about style. You haven't even seen a charade once in your lives! What is a programme without a charade? I'm merely asking you. Now listen to what I have to say to you! Taking part in a programme means giving one's best and now I propose to show my friend the Ancestor. He is not tired. He's not weak at the knees. He's angry!'

While Grandpa-Grumble was talking, Fillyjonk was seeing to the serving of the Welsh rarebits, discreetly, but doing it all the same. Grandpa-Grumble followed each Welsh rarebit as it arrived with his eyes, saw them land up on their plates and then yelled: 'You're spoiling my turn!'

'Oh, I'm sorry,' said Fillyjonk, 'but they're *hot*, they've just come out of the oven . . .'

'Bring them with you, bring them with you,' said Grandpa-Grumble impatiently. 'But hide them behind your backs so that he won't feel even more hurt. And take your glasses, too, so that you can drink his health.'

*

Fillyjonk held up a paper lantern and Grandpa-Grumble opened the clothes-cupboard. He bowed deeply. The Ancestor bowed, too.

'I can't be bothered to introduce them all to you,' Grandpa-Grumble said. 'You'd forget their names, and it's not all that important anyway.' He held out his glass towards the Ancestor and it clinked as they drank each other's health.

'But I don't understand,' exclaimed the Hemulen.

Mymble kicked him in the leg.

'You must all drink his health,' said Grandpa-Grumble, and stepped to one side. 'Where did he go to?'

'We're much too young to drink with him,' said Fillyjonk hastily, 'he might be angry . . .'

'Three cheers for the Ancestor!' the Hemulen exclaimed. 'One, two, three, hip hip hooray!'

As they were going back to the kitchen, Grandpa-Grumble turned to Fillyjonk and said: 'You're not all that young . . .'

'Yes, yes,' said Fillyjonk absently, and lifted her nose and sniffed. There was a musty smell, a nasty smell of decay. She looked at Toft. He turned away and thought: electricity.

It was nice to be back in the warm kitchen again.

'Now I want to see some conjuring tricks,' Grandpa-Grumble declared. 'Can anyone produce a rabbit out of my hat?'

128

'No, it's my turn now,' said Fillyjonk with dignity.

'I know what it is,' cried Mymble. 'It's going to be that awful business of hers where one of the guests goes out of the room and is eaten up, and then another goes outside and is eaten up . . .'

'It's a shadow-play,' said Fillyjonk unmoved. She went up to the stove and turned and faced them. 'It is a shadow-play, called "The Return".' She hung the sheet over the bread-rack in the ceiling. Then she placed the kitchen lamp on the log-basket behind the sheet and went round blowing out the lanterns one after the other.

'And when the lights went on again, the last one had been eaten up,' Mymble said under her breath.

The Hemulen hushed her. Fillyjonk disappeared behind the sheet, shining big and white, everybody looked and waited and Snufkin started to play softly, almost in a whisper.

Then a shadow appeared on the white sheet, a black silhouette, it was a boat. There was somebody very small sitting in the prow who had an onion-shaped little knot on top of her head.

It's Little My, Mymble thought. She looks just like that. I must say this is well done.

The boat glided slowly on across the sheet, over the sea, never before had a boat sailed so silently and so naturally, and there sat the whole family, Moomintroll and Moominmamma with her handbag leaning against the gunwale and Moominpappa with his hat on sat in the stern and steered; they were sailing home. (But the rudder didn't look right.)

Toft could only look at Moominmamma. He had time to take in every detail, for him the dark shadow took on colours, the silhouettes seemed to move and all the time

Snufkin went on playing so fittingly that no one was conscious of the music until it stopped. The family had come home.

That was a real shadow-play, Grandpa-Grumble said to himself. I have seen many shadow-plays in my time and I can remember them all, but that was the best.

The curtain came down, the play was over. Fillyjonk blew out the kitchen lamp and the room was plunged in darkness. They all sat still in the dark, waiting, a little taken aback.

Suddenly Fillyjonk said: 'I can't find the matches.'

The darkness immediately took on a different character. They could hear the wind whistling, and it seemed as though the kitchen had expanded, the walls sliding out into the night beyond, and their legs felt cold.

'I can't find the matches!' Fillyjonk repeated shrilly.

There was a scraping of chair legs and something fell over on the table. They had all stood up, they bumped into each other in the dark, somebody got all tangled up in the sheet and fell over a chair. Toft raised his head, the Creature was outside now, a great heavy body rubbing along the wall by the kitchen door. There was a rumble of thunder.

'They're outside!' Fillyjonk screamed. 'They're crawling in here!'

Toft put his ear against the door and listened, he couldn't hear anything except the wind. He raised the latch and went out, and the door closed noiselessly behind him.

At last the lamp was alight. Snufkin had found the matches. The Hemulen gave an embarrassed laugh. 'Look!' he said, 'I've stuck my paw into the Welsh rarebit!'

The kitchen looked normal again, but no one sat down. And no one noticed that Toft wasn't there.

'We'll leave things just as they are,' said Fillyjonk nervously. 'Don't move anything, I'll wash up in the morning.'

'But you don't mean you're going home?' Grandpa-Grumble exclaimed. 'The Ancestor has gone to bed and now the fun can begin!'

But no one felt like going on with the party. They said good night to each other, hastily and very politely, shook paws, and in a little while all the guests had disappeared. Grandpa-Grumble stamped on the floor before he left. He said: 'Well, I was the last to leave at any rate!'

*

When Toft got outside in the darkness he stood and waited on the steps. The sky was a little lighter than the mountains, whose undulating contours rose above Moominvalley. The Creature was silent, but Toft knew that it was looking at him.

131

Toft called softly: 'Nummulite ... little Radiolaria, Protozoa ...' But it couldn't recognize the strange names in the book. It was probably just bewildered and didn't even know why it growled.

Toft was more worried than afraid. He was uneasy about what the Nummulite might do on its own, it was too big and too angry and not used to being either big or angry. He took an uncertain step and felt that the Creature immediately moved backwards.

'You needn't go,' Toft explained. 'Just move a little farther away.' He continued over the grass and the Creature retreated, a clumsy, shapeless shadow, the bushes cracked and snapped where the Creature passed.

It has become too big, Toft thought. It's so big that it can't move properly.

There were cracking sounds from the jasmine-bush. Toft stopped and whispered: 'Take it easy, easy ...'

The Creature growled at him. He could hear the faint

swish of the rain, the thunder was a long way away now. They went on. Toft talked softly all the time to his Creature. They arrived at the crystal ball, tonight it was clear blue and the heavy swell could be seen quite clearly in its depths.

'It's no good,' said Toft. 'We can't hit back. Neither of us will ever learn to hit back. You must believe me.'

The Nummulite listened, perhaps it was only listening to Toft's voice. He was cold and his shoes were wet, he grew impatient and said: 'Make yourself tiny and hide yourself! You'll never get through this!'

And suddenly the crystal ball became overshadowed. A dizzy vortex opened in the heavy blue swell and then closed itself again, the Creature of the Protozoa group had made itself tiny and returned to its proper element. Moominpappa's crystal ball, which gathered everything and took care of everything, had opened up for the bewildered Nummulite.

Toft went back to the house and crept up to his box-room. He curled up in the roach-net and went to sleep straight away.

*

After the others had all left, Fillyjonk remained standing in the middle of the floor, lost in thought. Everything was upside down, the streamers had been trodden on, the chairs overturned and the lanterns had dripped candlewax over everything. She picked up a Welsh rarebit off the floor, bit a piece off distractedly and threw the rest in the rubbish bucket. A successful party, she said to herself.

It was raining outside. She listened carefully but could hear only the rain. They had disappeared.

Actually, Fillyjonk was neither happy nor upset and not

a little bit tired. It was as though everything had come to a standstill, and she went on listening. Snufkin had left his mouth-organ on the table, she picked it up, held it in her paw and waited. There was only the rain outside. She raised the mouth-organ and blew into it, she moved it backwards and forwards listening to the sound. She sat down at the kitchen table. How did it go? Toodledi, toodledoo . . . It was difficult to get it right, she tried and tried again, moved very carefully from one note to the next and found the right one, the next came of its own accord. The tune slipped past her, but then came back. Obviously one had to feel for it, not search here and there. Toodledoo, toodledi, a whole string of notes came, each undeniably in the right place.

Hour after hour Fillyjonk sat at the kitchen table playing the mouth-organ, tentatively but with great devotion. The notes began to resemble tunes and the tunes became music. She played Snufkin's songs and she played her own; she couldn't be got at, nothing could make her feel unsafe now. She didn't worry whether the others could hear her or not. Outside in the garden all was quiet, all the creepy-crawly things had disappeared, and it was an ordinary dark autumn night with a rising wind.

Fillyjonk went to sleep at the kitchen table with her arms under her head. She slept very well until half past eight in the morning, and when she woke up she looked round and said to herself: what a mess! Today we're going to have a thorough clean-up!

CHAPTER 19

First Snow

AT eight thirty-five, with the morning still quite shrouded in darkness, all the windows were flung open one after the other, mattresses, bedcovers and blankets poured out over every window-sill and a wonderful draught rushed through the house and raised the dust in thick clouds.

Fillyjonk was cleaning. Every single pan was on the stove heating water, brushes and rags and bowls were dancing out of their cupboards and the veranda railings were decorated with carpets. It was an enormous cleaning up, the most enormous that anyone had ever seen. The others stood on the slope outside in amazement, watching Fillyjonk going in and out, backwards and forwards, with a scarf round her head and Moominmamma's apron on, which was so big that it went round her three times.

Snufkin went into the kitchen looking for his mouth-organ.

'It's on the shelf above the stove,' said Fillyjonk as she went past. 'I have been very careful with it.'

'You can keep it a little longer if you want,' said Snufkin uncertainly.

Fillyjonk answered in a matter-of-fact way: 'Take it. I'll get one of my own. And watch out, you're treading in the sweepings.'

It was wonderful to be cleaning again. She knew exactly where the dust had hidden itself; soft and grey and self-satisfied it had made itself comfortable in the corners; she searched out every single bit of fluff which had rolled itself into big fat balls full of hairs and thought it was safe, ha ha! Moth-larvae, spiders, centipedes, all kinds of creepy-crawlies were routed out by Fillyjonk's big broom, and lovely streams of hot water and soapy lather washed every-thing away, and it was by no means an inconsiderable amount of mess that went out of the door, bucketful after bucketful; it was really fun to be alive!

'I've never liked it when the womenfolk clean up,' said Grandpa-Grumble. 'Has anyone told her not to touch the Ancestor's clothes-cupboard?'

But the clothes-cupboard was cleaned, too, it had twice as big a cleaning as all the rest. The only thing that Filly-jonk didn't touch was the mirror inside the cupboard, she let that stay misty.

After a while, the fun of cleaning became contagious, and everybody except Grandpa-Grumble joined in. They carried water and shook carpets, they scrubbed a bit of floor here and there, they each had a window to clean and when they felt hungry they went into the pantry and looked for what was left over from the party. Fillyjonk didn't eat anything and she didn't talk, how on earth should she have time or inclination for things like that! Sometimes she whistled a little, she was light on her feet and moved like the wind – one moment here another there, she made up

for all her desolation and fright and thought casually: whatever took possession of me? I have been nothing better than a great big ball of fluff . . . and why? But she couldn't remember.

And so the wonderful day of the great cleaning came to a close, and, thank goodness, without rain. When dusk came everything was straight again, everything was clean, polished, aired and the house stared in surprise in all directions through its freshly-cleaned windows. Fillyjonk took off her scarf and hung Moominmamma's apron on its peg.

'That's that,' she said. 'And now I'm going home to clean my own place. It needs it.'

They sat on the veranda steps together, it was very cold in the evenings now, but a feeling of approaching change and departure kept them sitting there.

'Thanks for cleaning the house,' said the Hemulen in a voice filled with sincere admiration.

'Don't thank me,' Fillyjonk answered. 'I couldn't stop myself! You ought to do the same. Mymble, I mean.'

'There's one thing that's funny,' said the Hemulen. 'Sometimes I feel that everything we say and do and every-

138

thing that happens has happened once before, eh? If you understand what I mean. Everything is the same.'

'And why should it be different?' Mymble asked. 'A hemulen is always a hemulen and the same things happen to him all the time. With mymbles it sometimes happens that they run away in order to get out of the cleaning!' She laughed loudly and slapped her knees.

'Will you always be the same?' Fillyjonk asked her out of curiosity.

'I certainly hope so!' Mymble answered.

Grandpa-Grumble looked from one to the other, he was very tired of their cleaning and their talk about things which didn't make anything seem more real. 'It's cold here,' he said. He got up stiffly and went into the house.

'It's going to snow,' Snufkin said.

*

It snowed for the first time the next morning, small, hard flakes, and it was horribly cold. Fillyjonk and Mymble stood on the bridge and said good-bye. Grandpa-Grumble had still not yet woken up.

*

'This has been a very rewarding time,' said the Hemulen. 'I hope we shall meet again with the family.'

'Yes, yes,' said Fillyjonk absently. 'In any case, say that the china vase is from me. What's the name of that mouth-organ?'

'Harmonium Two,' said Snufkin.

'Have a nice journey,' Toft mumbled. And Mymble said: 'Give Grandpa-Grumble a kiss on the nose from me. And remember that he likes gherkins and that the river is a brook!'

Fillyjonk picked up her suitcase. 'See that he takes his medicine,' she said severely. 'Whether he wants to or not. A hundred years aren't to be taken lightly. And you can have a party now and then if you want.' She went on across the bridge without turning round. They disappeared in the swirling snow, lost in that mixed feeling of melancholy and relief that usually accompanies good-byes.

*

It snowed all day and got even colder. The snow-covered ground, the departure, the clean house – all gave the day a feeling of immobility and reflection. The Hemulen stood looking up at his tree, sawed off a bit of plank but let it lie on the ground. Then he stood and just looked. Sometimes he went and tapped the barometer.

Grandpa-Grumble lay on the drawing-room sofa and meditated upon the way things had changed. Mymble was right. Quite suddenly he had discovered that the brook was a stream, a brown stream curving past snowy banks and quite simply a brown stream. Now there was no point in fishing any longer. He put the velvet cushion over his head and recalled his own happy brook, he remembered more and more about it, and how the days passed long, long ago when there were lots of fish and nights were warm and light, and things happened all the time. One ran oneself off one's legs so as not to miss anything that happened, sometimes taking a little nap as an afterthought, and laughing at everything . . . He went to talk to the Ancestor. 'Hallo,' he said. 'It's snowing. Why do only little things happen nowadays? Why are they so trivial? Where is my brook?' Grandpa-Grumble was silent. He was tired of talking to a friend who never answered. 'You are too old,' he said, and thumped on the floor with his stick. 'And now that the

winter has come you'll get even older. One gets terribly old
in the winter.' Grandpa-Grumble looked at his friend and
waited. All the doors were open and the rooms were bare
and clean, all the cheerful sloppiness had gone, the carpets
lay fair and square in their rectangles, and it was cold and
the snowy winter light fell on everything, Grandpa-
Grumble suddenly felt angry and forlorn and shouted:
'What? Say something!' But the Ancestor didn't answer,
but stood there gaping in his dressing-gown, which was too
long for him, and didn't say a word.

'Come out of your cupboard,' said Grandpa-Grumble
sharply. 'Come out and have a look. They've changed
everything and we're the only two who know what things

were like at the beginning.' Then Grandpa-Grumble poked the Ancestor in the stomach with his stick rather violently. There was a tinkling sound and the old mirror fell apart and crashed to the floor, a single long narrow splinter pausing momentarily on the Ancestor's bewildered face – and it fell, too, and Grandpa-Grumble stood face to face with a sheet of brown cardboard that meant absolutely nothing to him.

'Oh, indeed, it's like that is it?' said Grandpa-Grumble. 'He's gone. He got angry and left.'

*

Grandpa-Grumble sat in front of the kitchen stove thinking. The Hemulen was sitting at the table with a lot of drawings spread out in front of him. 'Something's not right about the walls,' he said. 'They're crooked in the wrong way and you just fall through them. It's absolutely impossible to get them to fit the branches.'

Perhaps he went into hibernation, Grandpa-Grumble thought.

'As a matter of fact,' the Hemulen went on, 'walls just shut one in. If you sit in a tree perhaps it's nicer after all to see what's going on around you, what?'

Perhaps the important things happen in the spring, Grandpa-Grumble said to himself.

'What do you think?' the Hemulen asked. '*Is* it nicer?'

'No,' Grandpa-Grumble said. He hadn't been listening. At last he knew what he would do, it was quite simple! He would skip over the whole winter and with a single leap find himself in April. There was nothing worth bothering about, absolutely nothing! All he had to do was make a nice hole to sleep in for himself and let the world go by. When he woke up again everything would be as it should be. Grandpa-Grumble went into the pantry and took down the bowl with the spruce-needles, he was very happy and suddenly terribly sleepy. He walked past the brooding Hemulen and said: 'Bye-bye, I'm going to hibernate.'

*

That night the sky was completely clear. The thin ice crunched beneath Toft's paws as he walked through the garden. The valley was full of the silence of the cold and the snow shone on the hill slopes. The crystal ball was empty. It was nothing more than a pretty crystal ball. But the black sky was full of stars, millions of sparkling glittering diamonds, winter stars shimmering with the cold.

'It's winter now,' said Toft as he came into the kitchen.

The Hemulen had decided that the house would be nicer without walls, just a floor, and he bundled his papers together with a feeling of relief and said: 'Grandpa-Grumble has hibernated.'

'Has he got all his things with him?' Toft asked.

'What does he need them for?' the Hemulen said in surprise.

Of course, when you hibernate you're much younger when you wake up, and you don't need anything but to be left in peace. But Toft imagined that when one wakes up it's important to know that someone had thought about one while one has been sleeping. So he looked for Grandpa-Grumble's things and put them outside the clothes-cupboard. He covered Grandpa-Grumble with the eiderdown and tucked him up properly, the winter might be cold. The clothes-cupboard smelt faintly of spices. There was just enough brandy left for a refreshing thimbleful in April.

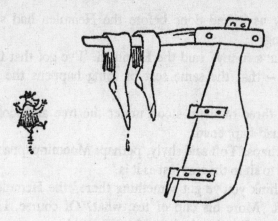

CHAPTER 20

Going Home

THE valley seemed even more silent after Grandpa-Grumble had gone into hibernation. Now and then the sound of the Hemulen hammering away up in the maple-tree could be heard. Sometimes he was chopping wood outside the woodshed. Otherwise everything was quiet. They said 'Hallo' and 'Good morning' to each other but they didn't feel like talking. They were waiting for their story to come to an end.

From time to time one of them went into the pantry to get something to eat. The coffee-pot stood on the stove all day keeping warm.

Actually, the silence in the valley was very beautiful, and restful, too, and they got used to each other much better by not meeting so often. The crystal ball was completely empty, and ready to be filled up by whatever might come. It got colder and colder all the time.

One morning something happened. The floor of the tree-house fell out with a crash and the maple-tree looked exactly as it had done before the Hemulen had started building.

'That's funny,' said the Hemulen. 'I've got that feeling again – that the same sort of thing happens the whole time.'

All three of them stood under the tree and looked at what had happened.

'Perhaps,' Toft said shyly, 'perhaps Moominpappa would prefer to sit in the tree just as it is.'

'I think you've got something there,' the Hemulen admitted. 'More his cup of tea, what? Of course, I could knock a nail in for the lamp, but it would seem more natural if it hung on a branch.'

They went inside to have coffee, and this time they drank it together and had saucers as well as cups.

'Imagine us being brought together by an accident,' the Hemulen said gravely and stirred his coffee. 'And what shall we do now?'

'Wait,' said Toft.

'Of course,' said the Hemulen, 'but what about me? All you need to do is wait until they get back, but it's a different matter for me.'

'Why?' Toft asked.

'I don't know,' said the Hemulen.

Snufkin poured out some more coffee and said: 'The wind will get up after twelve o'clock.'

'That's the sort of thing you're always saying!' Toft burst out. 'Someone asks what he's got to do, and what will happen, and this is awful, and all you can say is that it's going to snow, or there'll be a storm or something, or do you want some more sugar . . .'

'You're angry again,' said the Hemulen in surprise. 'Why are you only angry at such long intervals?'

'I don't know,' Toft muttered. 'I'm not angry, it just comes over me . . .'

'I was thinking of the dinghy,' Snufkin explained. 'If the wind gets up after twelve o'clock, the Hemulen and I could go out for a sail.'

'The boat leaks,' the Hemulen said.

'No it doesn't,' said Snufkin. 'I've made it tight. And I found the sail in the woodshed. Do you want to come sailing?'

Toft hastily cast his eyes down at his coffee-cup, he knew that the Hemulen was scared. And the Hemulen said: 'It would be absolutely wonderful.'

*

The wind got up round half past one, not very much, but there were tiny white horses all over the sea. Snufkin had the dinghy waiting at the bathing-hut jetty, he raised the spritsail and let the Hemulen sit in the bow. It was very cold and they were wearing all the woollen things they could find. The sky was clear, with a bank of dark-blue wintry clouds over the horizon. Snufkin turned out towards the point, the dinghy heeled over and gathered speed.

'The majesty of the sea,' the Hemulen cried in a tremulous voice, his nose was pale and he stared in horror at the leeward gunwale, it was much too close to the frothing green sea. So this is how it feels, he thought. This is what sailing is like. The world turns upside down and you hang on for dear life to the edge of the yawning abyss, you freeze and feel ashamed and when it's too late you wish you'd never come. Let's hope and pray he doesn't notice how scared I am.

Just beyond the point the dinghy ran into the heavy swell from some storm out at sea. Snufkin tacked and continued farther out.

The Hemulen began to feel sick. It came slowly, treacherously, he yawned and yawned and swallowed and swallowed, and suddenly he felt weak and wretched all over his body, and a nasty sick feeling rose from his stomach. He just wanted to die.

'Now you take the rudder,' said Snufkin.

'No, no, no,' the Hemulen whispered, feebly waving his paws in protest, but the movement started more ghastly torture in his stomach and the whole of the merciless sea revolved in the other direction.

'You must take the rudder,' Snufkin repeated. He got up and scrambled across to the middle thwart. The rudder swung to and fro on its own, helplessly – someone had to catch hold of it, this was awful – the Hemulen moved astern, he stumbled and staggered over the thwarts and grabbed the rudder with his frozen paws, the sail swung wildly, it was the end of the world! And Snufkin just sat and stared at the horizon.

The Hemulen steered this way and that, the sail creaked, and water came into the dinghy, and Snufkin went on staring at the horizon. The Hemulen felt so sick that he couldn't even think, so he steered by instinct, and suddenly he could steer, the sail filled with wind and the dinghy set course along the coast in the heavy swell.

Now I won't be sick, the Hemulen thought. I'll hold on to the rudder as hard as I can and I won't be sick.

His stomach began to settle. He kept his eyes riveted on the bow, which rose up and down, and the dinghy sailed free with the wind farther and farther out to sea.

*

Toft had done the washing-up and made the Hemulen's bed. He had gathered together the floor-boards under the maple-tree and hidden them behind the woodshed. Now he was sitting at the kitchen table, listening to the wind and waiting.

At last he heard them talking in the garden, they had got back. He heard steps outside the kitchen and the Hemulen came in and said: 'Hallo.'

'Hallo,' said Toft. 'Was it blowy?'

'A strong gale,' the Hemulen answered. 'Fresh, rough weather.' He was still green in the face and so cold that he was shaking all over, he took off his boots and socks and hung them on the stove to dry. Toft poured out some coffee for him. They sat opposite each other at the table and felt embarrassed.

'I wonder,' said the Hemulen, 'I wonder whether it won't soon be about time to go home.' He sneezed, and added: 'I did the steering.'

'Perhaps you're homesick for your boat,' Toft muttered.

The Hemulen was silent for a long time. When he eventually spoke he had a look of tremendous relief on his face. 'You know what,' he said, 'I'll tell you something. It was the first time in my whole life that I have ever been out at sea.'

Toft didn't look up, and the Hemulen asked: 'Aren't you surprised?'

Toft shook his head.

The Hemulen got up and started to walk up and down the kitchen, he was very excited. 'I thought sailing was ghastly,' he said. 'I felt so sick that all I wanted to do was die, and I was scared the whole time!'

Toft looked at the Hemulen and said: 'It must have been awful.'

'It was,' the Hemulen agreed gratefully. 'But I didn't let Snufkin notice anything! He thought I was good at holding

the sail, I had the right touch. And now I know I don't have to sail. Funny, isn't it, eh? I've just realized I don't ever need to sail again.' The Hemulen raised his head and laughed heartily. He blew his nose violently in the kitchen towel and said: 'I'm warm again now. As soon as my boots and socks are dry I'm going home. I'm sure everything's in a mess there! Lots to get organized!'

'Will you do the cleaning?' Toft asked.

'Of course not!' the Hemulen exclaimed. 'I shall arrange things for other people. There aren't many people who know how they should live and can manage on their own!'

*

The bridge had always been the place for good-byes. The Hemulen's boots and socks were dry and he was ready to leave. The wind was still blowing and his thin hair was all over the place. He had caught a cold, or perhaps it was just emotion.

'Here's my poem,' said the Hemulen, giving Snufkin a piece of paper. 'I have written it out as a memento. You know, the one that starts "Where lies true lasting happiness". Bless you, and say hallo to the family for me.' He waved his paw and left.

Just as the Hemulen had crossed the bridge, Toft came running after him and asked: 'What are you going to do with your boat?'

'My boat?' the Hemulen repeated. 'Oh yes, my boat.'

He thought and then said: 'I shall wait until I meet a suitable person.'

'You mean somebody who dreams of sailing,' Toft said.

'Not at all!' the Hemulen answered. 'Someone who

needs a boat.' He waved his paw again and disappeared among the birch-trees.

Toft heaved a sigh of relief. One more left. Soon the valley would be as empty as the crystal ball and would belong to no one except the Moomin family and Toft. He passed Snufkin and asked: 'When are you off?'

'It all depends,' Snufkin answered.

CHAPTER 21

Coming Home

TOFT went into Moominmamma's room for the first time. It was white. He filled the water-jug and smoothed out the crocheted bedcover. He put Fillyjonk's vase on the bedside table. Moominmamma had no pictures on the walls and on the desk there was only a small dish with safety-pins, a rubber cork and two round stones. On the window-sill Toft found a clasp-knife. She forgot it, he thought. That's the one she usually makes little boats out of bark with. But perhaps she had another one with her. He pulled out the blades, the big one and the small one, they were both quite blunt and the awl was broken off. There was a tiny pair of scissors attached to the knife, but she hadn't used them much. Toft went out to the woodshed and sharpened the knife. Then he put it back on the window-sill.

The weather had suddenly become milder, and the wind changed to south-west. That's the family's wind. I know they like the wind from the south-west best, Toft thought.

A bank of clouds slowly accumulated over the sea, and the whole sky became heavy with them and it was easy to see that they were full of snow. Within a few days all the

153

valleys would be covered with winter, they had been waiting for it for a long time, but now it was on its way.

Snufkin stood outside his tent and knew that it was time to break camp, he was ready to be off. The valley would soon be cut off.

Slowly and calmly he pulled up the pegs and rolled up the tent. He doused the fire. He was in no hurry today.

Everything was empty and clean, all that was left was a rectangle of bleached grass showing where he had lived. The snow would cover that up, too, the next day.

He wrote a letter to Moomintroll and put it into the letter-box. His rucksack was already packed and waiting on the bridge.

At first light Snufkin went to the beach to fetch his five bars of music. He climbed over the banks of seaweed and driftwood and stood on the sand waiting. They came immediately and they were more beautiful and even simpler than he had hoped they would be.

Snufkin went back to the bridge as the song about the rain got nearer and nearer, he slung his rucksack over his shoulders and walked straight into the forest.

*

That evening a tiny but steady light was shining in the crystal ball. The family had hung the storm-lantern at the top of the mast and they were on their way home to hibernate for the winter.

The south-west wind was still blowing and the bank of clouds had risen high in the sky. There was a smell of snow in the air, a heavy, clean smell.

*

Toft wasn't surprised when he saw that the tent had gone. Perhaps Snufkin had understood that Toft was the only one who should meet the family when they got home. For an instant, Toft wondered whether Snufkin perhaps understood a great deal more than one would think – but only for an instant. Then Toft began thinking about himself again. His dream about meeting the family again had become so enormous that it made him feel tired. Every time he thought about Moominmamma he got a headache. She had grown so perfect and gentle and consoling that it was unbearable, she was a big, round smooth balloon without a face. The whole of Moominvalley had somehow become unreal, the house, the garden and the river were nothing but a play of shadows on the screen and Toft no longer knew what was real and what was only his imagination. He had been made to wait too long and now he was angry. He sat on the kitchen steps hugging his knees and kept his eyes tight shut, huge strange pictures crowded into his head and suddenly he was scared! He jumped up and started running, he ran past the kitchen-garden, the rubbish-heap, straight into the forest and all of a sudden it was dark, he was in the waste ground, the ugly abandoned forest that Mymble had talked about. Inside there was perpetual dusk. The trees stood uneasily close to one another, there wasn't enough room for their branches, and they were all quite thin. The ground looked like wet leather. The only things that glistened were the flame-coloured finger-tip mushrooms growing like small hands out of the dark, and on the tree trunks there were great mouldy lumps looking like cream and white velvet. It was a different world. Toft had no pictures and no words for it, nothing had to correspond. No one had tried to make a path here and no one had ever rested under the trees. They had just walked

around with sinister thoughts, this was the forest of anger. He grew quite calm and very attentive. With enormous relief the worried Toft felt all his pictures disappear. His descriptions of the valley and the Happy Family faded and slipped away, Moominmamma glided away and became remote, an impersonal picture, he didn't even know what she looked like.

Toft walked on through the forest, stooping under the branches, creeping and crawling, and thinking of nothing at all and became as empty as the crystal ball. This is where Moominmamma had walked when she was tired and cross and disappointed and wanted to be on her own, wandering

aimlessly in the endless forest lost in her dejection . . . Toft
saw an entirely new Moominmamma and she seemed natural to him. He suddenly wondered why she had been unhappy and whether there was anything one could do about
it.

The forest began to thin out and huge grey mountains
lay in front of him. They were covered with depressions
full of boggy ground almost to their peaks, where they rose
big and completely bare. Up there was nothing, just the
wind. The sky was vast, and full of great scurrying snow-
clouds. Everything was enormous. Toft looked behind him
and the valley was just an insignificant shadow below him.
Then he looked at the sea.

The whole sea lay spread out in front of him, grey and
streaked with even white waves right out to the horizon.
Toft turned his face into the wind and sat down to wait.

Now, at last, he could wait.

The family had the wind with them and they were
making straight for the shore. They were coming from
some island where Toft had never been and which
he couldn't see. Perhaps they felt like staying there,
he thought. Perhaps they will make up a story about
that island and tell it to themselves before they go to
sleep.

Toft sat high up on the mountain for several hours looking at the sea.

Just before the sun went down it threw a shaft of light
through the clouds, cold and wintry-yellow, making the
whole world look very desolate.

And then Toft saw the storm-lantern Moominpappa
had hung up at the top of the mast. It threw a gentle, warm
light and burnt steadily. The boat was a very long way
away. Toft had plenty of time to go down through the

forest and along the beach to the jetty, and be just in time
to catch the line and tie up the boat.

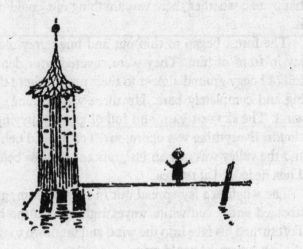

It all started with a Scarecrow

Puffin is well over sixty years old.
Sounds ancient, doesn't it? But Puffin has never been
so lively. We're always on the lookout for the next big
idea, which is how it began all those years ago.

Penguin Books was a big idea from the mind of
a man called Allen Lane, who in 1935 invented
the quality paperback and changed the world.
**And from great Penguins, great Puffins grew,
changing the face of children's books forever.**

The first four Puffin Picture Books were hatched in 1940 and the
first Puffin story book featured a man with broomstick arms called
Worzel Gummidge. In 1967 Kaye Webb, Puffin Editor, started the
Puffin Club, promising to **'make children into readers'**.
She kept that promise and over 200,000 children became
devoted Puffineers through their quarterly installments of
Puffin Post, which is now back for a new generation.

Many years from now, we hope you'll look back and
remember Puffin with a smile. **No matter what your age
or what you're into, there's a Puffin for everyone.**
The possibilities are endless, but one thing is for sure:
whether it's a picture book or a paperback, a sticker book
or a hardback, **if it's got that little Puffin
on it – it's bound to be good.**